Off-License To Kill
A James Vagabond Adventure
by Aug Stone

First Printing: 2015

ISBN 978-1-329-61986-9

www.augstone.com

Cover art by Jodie Lowther

Special thanks to Alex Sarll for the subediting expertise, Jodie for the cover, and Benjamin Haas and Judi DeCicco for the encouragement

Dedicated to
Paul Haswell, Clare Best, Nichola Halliday, Julia Boyce,
& the memory of The Strange Fruit Collective, London, 2003

1 – Something's Brewing

"And you know whose effing fault that is!"

James Vagabond stopped short in his walk down Leidestraat, just past where the insane-looking man sat clutching the edge of the bench, both hands gripped white, with wine-reddened face nearly screaming near-obscenities. Vagabond missed whose fault it was as he paused to consider. Yes, the man had said 'effing'. The ranting, the ratty clothes, the stench of stale alcohol were all there, along with the loud speech that was not yet a yell, and the toning down of any offensive language so as not to draw too much attention to himself or disrupt the public – this man might be a fellow agent. Vagabond scratched his abundant brown beard as he turned slowly around, strolled behind the man, and sat down on the opposite end of the bench. His begrimed jacket falling open to reveal filthy threadbare formalwear, an unkempt gentleman right down to his boots thick with soot. Outwardly oblivious to James' proximity, the man intoned "Gherkin!" and kicked the air in front of him. James would have to be patient; if this man was an agent of his Service he would make himself known in due time. There was no protocol for James to approach the tramp himself, this sort of thing was not done. Besides, James had no idea why he would need to be contacted, here in Amsterdam, during his three weeks leave. But something was surely amiss, he could sense it in the air, taste it in this morning's beer. James began scouring the ground for cigarette butts to pass the time. Finding fifteen smokeable ends, he placed one in his mouth and the other fourteen into his left-hand coat pocket, the pocket without the siphoning hole inside. Now there was the problem of lighting this tiny amount of tobacco. The insane man next to him, currently babbling an incomprehensible incantation about the ancient Inca civilisation, continued to ignore James' presence at the other end of the bench. To ask a passerby would be risky, most did not take kindly to James' kind. His eyes roamed the pavement for discarded yet still flame-worthy matches or, even better, a lost lighter, but to no avail. Approaching panic, James began searching frantically about his person, an epileptic pantomime of a baboon scratching itself, and many pedestrians quickened their paces as they went by the now two insane-looking men on the bench. After a minute, James pulled a disheveled matchbook out of his right sock. It nearly disintegrated in his fingers as he fervently hoped it could still produce fire, soggy as it was from so much accumulated sweat. As the sickly flame danced to celebrate his luck, James sat back to enjoy his second-hand cigarette butt.

The unhinged hobo now launched into a tirade about a 'physics scam' and James decided to take his coat off and relax a little. It would be good to let the dirt-, food-, and alcohol-stained jacket air out. He took another cigarette butt, lit it off the one he was smoking, and watched the pigeons pecking along the ground. He felt triumphant over them with his bounty of smokes and thought about lighting two or three at once, just to rub the birds' beaks in his superiority. But kindness prevailing, he pulled some day-old food out of his beard and threw it to them. One good turn deserves another; maybe one of them would buy him a drink someday. He laughed that he was getting whimsical. Still no sign from his crazed companion. Reclining a bit more, he recalled the phrase 'Birds gather on empty ground' from chapter nine of Sun-Tzu's *The Art of War*. It had been compulsory reading for a class in his training days for the Service. The day after that lecture, the trainees were taken out to study how animals behaved under the influence of alcohol. Before the demonstration the students and instructors had gotten quite bevvied up themselves and James couldn't now remember if it had actually been required for them to observe drunken animals at all. Z Branch - when they weren't asleep - were currently experimenting with genetically engineering a mammal that would produce alcohol instead of milk. Beer-yielding bovine, Gin Bottlenosed Whales, Merlocelots, were all in the works.

James was growing bored and impatient. He half-heartedly listened to the madman's rants on 'the automobile and witchcraft', people who were actually fish and therefore shouldn't be allowed to smoke or enter certain restaurants, "even if they do both at the same time", and something called 'emotion sickness', hoping to pick up some sort of clue. Soon James' fellow tramp pulled out a pair of scissors and, trimming pieces off his own beard, attempted to beckon the pigeons with the hair between his fingers.

"Here birdie, here little birdie birdie, the hair that inspired Galileo…"

James lit another cigarette butt while the pigeons kept their distance. Unperturbed, their would-be summoner produced a piccolo flute from within his maze of rags. His fingers moved furiously over the keys, though a note would only sound every ten seconds or so, infuriating to anyone paying the least bit of attention.

James finally stood up to go, fidgeting back into his filthy jacket, but as he walked in front of the insane man, his benchmate casually looked up at him and offered a flask with the words, "Have a drink, sir." James' recognition of the ritual did not show on his grimy face but he answered in turn, "Thank you very much, my kind friend" and offered his hand to shake. This exchange was part of the official coded dialogue between members of the Service, changed monthly for reasons of security, and meant absolutely nothing at all. It was enacted to give a false scent to their enemies while the real way agents identified each other was by the bottle cap the man now pressed into James' hand. James unscrewed the top, moved the flask to his lips, and pretended to drink. For a second he held the container slightly in front of his face, looking at it as if to say 'My, that was refreshing!' and listened to the message intended for him. *Home at once.* He passed the flask back to the insane man and was on his way. The idea had come from the children's toy that when turned upside-down and then back up again would make a 'moo-ing' sound. It was always disappointing to put a flask to one's lips and have nothing come out but such were the demands of the job.

James quickly made his way to the backstreet where he had slept the past few nights, by far the most pleasing alleyway he had lodged in during his three weeks in Amsterdam. He grabbed the half-finished bottle of Jenever from under his nest of newspapers and set off for the Damrak. He had been told before he left for Amsterdam that if an emergency were to arise there would be a reservation awaiting him at Central Station for the Eurostar back to London. Vagabond felt uneasy about this, he would have preferred his normal means of travel, as a stowaway, but knew it would not be possible to organise ticketless transport in a hurry. He took a rejuvenating swig of the Jenever and reconciled himself to the idea of riding a train in, of all things, a seat.

Walking down the Damrak now, with the Red Light District to his right, James reflected on his past few weeks in this city of diamonds, canals, and Dutch courage. All the ladies who had opened their glass doors and said that he could come in for free, or the one, responsible for the newest rip in his jacket, who had pulled him in and taken advantage of him before he could even recap his bottle of Jenever. After three days of this, he had been so thoroughly worn out that he forced himself to stay away for two days to recover, concentrating solely on his drinking. One particular professional, however, found the alley where he was staying and would visit him at night when he was too drunk to put up much resistance. She even managed to find him when he switched sidestreets. And there had been the ill-chosen new sleeping spot that was too dark to see much of anything at all, and he really hoped in the morning that that had been her. He scratched now at his beard that held the ladies' accumulated lipstick prints as well as built-up dirt, food, and beer froth. He thought about going to say goodbye if there was enough time before his train. Maybe a lover would be waiting for him at the station for one last romp in the toilets. But no, they'd have no way of knowing, and going back to those glass palaces beside the canals would be too careless. He called himself back to his duties and quickened his pace towards Central Station. Something was definitely going on, something quite significant; he could smell it in the air.

There was a ticket waiting at the counter under the name of László Somerwine. He had just enough time to smoke two cigarette butts before he was due at the gate. The other passengers steered clear of him, sneering at his filthy, tattered rags and ultra-unkempt appearance with contempt. But passport control and the staff at each station had been given the bare minimum of information and he boarded the train without any hassle. He made his way to an empty seat, smiling politely at those pushing away from him. As he sat down, the few people remaining in the car were heard making excuses of "Yes, I'm hungry too, let's check on the restaurant car", the meal service James knew would not be open yet. Alone, and quite happy to be so, he snuggled into the corner and opened his bottle of Jenever. At least this connecting train was far less posh than the Eurostar, could even be considered run-down. He took the newspaper someone had left in a hurry on the seat next to him, covered himself with it, and closed his eyes. There would be an hour and a half layover in Bruxelles. James wished he had a way to contact that sexy Swedish spy, Cori Anderson, who was always stationed in Belgium, but alas he had neither the time nor the means. He resolved himself to once again trying to grow to like the spice they put in Belgian White Ale, each attempt a little more successful, although he was still not altogether used to it, nor could he yet sip without a wince. His next course of drinking now decided upon, he swigged the last of the Jenever, cursing himself that in his rush he had left the Tabasco that would complement its flavour so well under another paper back in the alley, and closed his eyes again.

The train pulled in to Bruxelles-Midi half an hour late and so James Vagabond's layover was cut down to only sixty minutes. He decided to play one of his favourite games at the station while he waited – draining a beer at every drinking establishment within view. Once committed to the game he shivered, remembering that, by his previous decision, it would have to be White Ale. As he tentatively tasted the first tall glass, his body and mind locked in battle. He knew he would have to drink quickly if he hoped to make it to every eligible location in only the hour he had. But he couldn't seem to swallow the stuff fast enough, his startled taste buds instinctively slowing him down. He thought about employing the common technique of just pouring the liquid straight down the throat, avoiding any sensation of taste, but his mind wrestled with itself on this question - the whole point of the exercise was to develop a taste for White Ale. He toyed with the idea of working with a drinking coach when he got back to his normal routine in London. He had found it necessary to employ this measure only once before and although it was a reasonable enough problem - some people just didn't like certain flavours - it was still an emasculating experience for any member of the Service to have to go through. I Branch, who handled this sort of thing, did quite a good job though, top secret - your prolonged absence from duty was disguised as 'the flu' or a 'special assignment'. James remembered the harrowing two weeks he had dealt with his Slivowicz problem – fourteen straight days of drinking that biting liqueur and eating only plums at meals. At first he had been allowed beer chasers but once those were taken away he suffered a total emotional breakdown. Upon completion of the course, however, a revitalised James Vagabond sent a message to D stating that if there was ever any need for an agent in the Czech Republic, he was the man.

He finished his first ale and moved quickly on to the next available tap, trying to make up time while traveling. For sipping his second suds, the effects of the half bottle of Jenever, the Irish coffee he had had for breakfast, and the previous beer combined to make this pint a little easier. He looked up at the Stella signs and recalled the last time he had played this game at Bruxelles-Midi, when he had managed seven in an hour. Seven Stellas in an hour! It reminded him of Amsterdam. Seven may not seem like too overwhelming a number but one must consider there are other factors at play in this game – progressing from drink station to drink station without arousing suspicion, waiting in the various lengthy queues, resisting the wiles of blondes supping blondes, etc. In the end he boarded the Eurostar having had four White Ales total, feeling neither pleased nor disappointed in himself, and not quite sure if he liked the taste of coriander in his drink any more than before.

James Vagabond awoke from a short nap to find himself in his comfortable Eurostar seating rushing towards the coast and the Chunnel. A ways to go yet. Someone, he presumed the man with the food and beverage cart, had left a can of Carlsberg on the seat next to him. He opened it thankfully and took a long pull. He sensed movement to his left and glanced across the aisle to see a sultry redhead eyeing him. She giggled playfully. He took another slug from the can and wondered if he had something obvious sticking out of his beard. Running his hand over his face, he found nothing. She winked at him and smiled. James looked over this sexy stranger more closely. Her full lips declined in a natural pout, her low-cut top revealed freckles jumping out of the sizeable cleavage. She jiggled a little then crossed her legs, shifting them in James' direction. James scanned the cabin; they seemed to be alone, naturally. Pulling down her black skirt a touch, she got up and took James' beer out of his hand, sitting herself on his lap. Quickly, before James could panic and yell 'Thief!', she put the can to his lips and he drank long and deep, finishing the remainder of the beverage. The mysterious woman tossed the can to the floor with abandon and kissed him passionately. She stood up again and took James' hand. Almost in a daze, he too arose and followed her down the aisle towards the next compartment.

James forced himself to concentrate. He did not recognise her as an enemy agent nor did she particularly look or act like she could possibly be one. She left an ample amount of space between them for James to view her well-shaped behind, like a cross section of a brandy snifter. The black stockings and heels excited him, though he quickly registered that they were not stilettos, nor could he see anything else about her person that might possibly be used as a weapon. She turned back and blew him a kiss, "Almost there."

James knew he must keep aware that this could be a trap, though he fervently hoped it wasn't. She had thrown the can to the ground and the only other possible protection he had on him was his ever-present bottle opener and corkscrew. He grasped it tightly in his coat pocket and in doing so felt the ten unsmoked cigarette butts. Well, if worst came to worst, a handful of disgusting filter tips thrown in the face could buy him a second or two. He wished he could get his jacket off, tossing that over her head might also provide time to escape, but the woman held his other hand too firmly.

"Here we are," she smiled and he felt his pulse quicken. He readied himself as she threw open the door. In front of him, spread out across the scented room, were ten gorgeous women in various states of undress. James let his eyes fall over three brunettes, two obviously dyed blondes, another redhead, two natural blondes, and one black-haired fox. As the door closed behind them, James, somewhat shocked and confused, told himself he could relax, as long as he stayed on guard.

"I'm Splendide," the lady who led him there began, "and this is Tastey, that's Licketey," she pointed to two twins, "over there is..." But James lost track of who was who as a dozen hands caressed him towards a fully stocked open cooler that seemed to be waiting especially for his arrival. The girl who had been introduced to him as Cookie took his hand and led him to a spot on the floor near a deck of cards, as the others closed in to form a circle.

"We're playing strip baccarat," she explained. "Won't you join us?"

Soon delighted screams of 'Oh James!' blended in with the rush of the train as it sped on towards London.

2 – D

Vagabond walked as quickly as he could through Waterloo Station towards his bus stop. The girls had thoroughly exhausted him but he knew he must hurry; it was unwise to keep D waiting. He couldn't appear in too much of a rush however, enemy agents might be watching. Putting as much elegant nonchalance as he could muster into his gait, he nevertheless still attracted looks of disgust from passersby. Under the crowded bus shelter James took a much-needed beer out of his pocket. He had managed to pilfer two from the girls' cooler as he was kissing them all goodbye. James now wondered why they hadn't offered any to him on his way out – a little rude, he thought. As he finished the can and placed it in the recycling bin, the 168 bus pulled up and people began to climb on. In his haste he hadn't realised that he didn't have any money on him and so began to scour the ground for the needed fare. He was kicked quite a few times by the other would-be-passengers trying to step on the bus, some accidentally, some on purpose, as he could tell by the comments that accompanied the boots. Looking up in dismay as the last of the commuters were boarding, James caught a friendly smile and was waved on. The driver tipped his hat to Vagabond and James realised that D would have known what time he was arriving at Waterloo and tipped off all buses within a fifteen-minute frame that James was to be expected. More relaxed now, James scanned the vehicle for any awaiting vixens and then for a place to sit. He was disappointed on both accounts, as he saw none of the former and a fellow disheveled-looking character scurrying into the last available seat near the back doors. James recognised this vagrant as a troublemaker, not at all connected with the Service. He clutched the remaining beer can concealed in his coat, thankful that it was in his left pocket, opposite the man, and would hopefully still be shielded from him on the turn up the stairs. He just had to stay calm.

Finding the first row of the upper deck to be unoccupied, James took a seat in the left corner. On second thought he moved to the aisle seat and took off his jacket, placing it on the seat to his left. He paused for a second, then slowly removed the beer can from his pocket, counted another second, then lightly pulled the tab up. He quickly thrust the opened beer can under his coat on the seat, folded his hands in his lap, and waited. Sure enough, after about twenty seconds, James caught a glimpse in the window of the dirty hat, scorched face, and hunting eyes peering around the staircase railings. James continued to look straight ahead as he watched the reflection of the tramp rise into full view, searching hungrily about the top floor with his eyes. And then, after what seemed like a very long time indeed, he moved off downstairs again with a grunt. Relieved, but still hesitant, James waited a full minute before turning around to see what the man had discovered. He smiled an unseen smile at the little girl drinking a soda next to her mother far in the back on the right. Turning again to the window, he kept an eye on the girl, and brought the can to his mouth only when she did, drinking for exactly the same duration, just in case the man downstairs heard the sips.

As he stepped off the bus in Camden Town, James was glad, for his sake, that the girl was a quick drinker. He had managed to finish his beer and leave the empty can under his seat, thereby avoiding a possible incident had he to carry it back off the bus, with the risk of it being smelt or angrily seen through the window as he commenced finishing it outside. James saw some old friends, including some fellow agents, at the intersection near the tube stop but sensing the immediacy of whatever situation had called him back to London, he put his head down and hastened towards the High Street.

Having passed Camden Lock about a minute ago, James smoothly turned off the main road and a few dozen steps later into the shop with the non-descript white Off-License sign hanging outside. The shop just after the doorway with, if one cared to notice, though no one ever did, a small plaque above its entrance that read 'XXX Port, 3rd Floor'. The London offices of the makers of the world's strongest fortified wine, that no one ever had any reason to visit – if a meeting with the 'directors' did need to be arranged, it was usually conducted at a hotel bar somewhere.

Bossa nova music blared as James waved to the faithful store clerk behind the counter.

"Afternoon, Boss".

The man known as 'Boss' saluted back. James grabbed two beers from the shelf as he walked towards the back of the shop and disappeared into the storeroom. A minute later a man dressed almost identically to James strolled out, took two beers off the shelf, nodded to Boss, and set off back towards Camden Town. This was the usual procedure of an agent reporting to headquarters – the decoy making it look like just an ordinary off-license. Meanwhile James descended through the trap door in the storeroom then over and up into the secret entrance door to the offices of XXX Port. He knocked, not too loudly, on the wall, and waited. Soon Miss Glassbottle, D's personal secretary, would let him in. The system worked well; if for some reason there was a visitor in the office who noticed the noise, Miss Glassbottle would remark on the walls being thin and that 'They make such an awful racket next door.' But there were hardly ever any outsiders in the office, and no one could think of a time when Miss Glassbottle had been required to use this excuse.

"Well hullo James, and how was your trip?"

"Splendid, Glassbottle. Splendid. Though I spent the whole time missing you," he smiled.

"In Amsterdam? I think not." Sashaying back behind her desk, she informed him "He'll be with you in a minute or so, James" and went back to reading her Bukowski book. Out of habit James grabbed a beer from one of the multiple refrigerators about the office and took a scat himself on the ratty couch in the corner.

James' eyes idly scanned the room. A new painting hung next to the door through which he had entered. Abhorring those portraits of misguided men and women dumping perfectly good alcohol into various harbors, the Service had taken to purchasing such so-called 'art' and touching them up. This fresh canvas depicted a raging sea, coloured deep red out to the horizon, with dozens of swimmers luxuriating in these fortified waters, the faces of those pouring the barrels of wine above altered to show supreme pleasure in the beneficence of their actions. James shifted his focus to Miss Glassbottle's haunting green eyes and sighed. Ah, Miss Glassbottle, who would drink you under the table and have her way with you there, all during lunch hour. Unlike Vagabond's own secretary, Miss Blush, or Rosé as he called her in their more intimate moments, who would literally drink you under the table, while you stayed in your chair.

Miss Glassbottle looked up and smiled back into Vagabond's eyes. "Not now, James," she laughed and went back to her reading. James practiced drinking with minimal amount of movement. You never knew when such economies just might save your life or your drinking arm. Soon the tap on the wall began to pour luminescent nectar down into the waiting gold pint glass on the table below it. When the amber liquid reached the top, the burgundy door at the far end of the room swung open. James Vagabond took the full glass and brought it in to D, the mastermind who controlled his country's Drunken Secret Service, the man responsible for keeping his compatriots drinking; the man with the golden glass.

"Good evening, Double-O Double-O. I trust your journey home was satisfactory?" he asked, motioning for James Vagabond to take a seat in front of his vast burgundy oak desk. He pushed the giant bowl - so large it took up a third of the surface of the stained leather tabletop - of discarded but still smokeable cigarette stubs, collected daily from the streets of Camden and Islington, towards James as he sat down. James stared into the mass of Grates, Cinders, and half-size-to-begin-with Cygnets; Sooties, Modern Mariners, and Olde Factorys; selected a Fumetti, and lit it with the pistol-shaped lighter next to the bowl. As he inhaled, James leant back and surveyed the familiar bookcases overflowing with rare bottles and their boxes, dirty glasses, and photos of famous drinkers, all obscuring ancient cocktail recipe books whose contents had long since been memorised.

"Splendid, sir. No trouble at all."

D smiled at his response.

"It appears we have a situation on our hands, Double-O Double-O," D took a cigarette end himself, along with a generous swig from his golden pint glass and continued, "Are you familiar with Prohibition, Double-O Double-O?"

"Um, I think so, sir. Do you mean what happened in America early last century? When they actually changed their Constitution to ban the manufacturing of alcohol?"

"That's it, Double-O Double-O. Amendment Eighteen to the United States Constitution, ratified January 1919. Luckily they had the good sense to repeal it with Amendment Twenty-One in December 1933. My, that's a long time. I still can't believe it went through in the first place. Drink changes the constitution enough as it is."

Vagabond sat looking puzzled for a moment. Taking another butt from the bowl, he waited for D to continue. When he did not, James remarked, "I'm sorry, sir, I don't quite see what this has to do with us."

"Certain people are getting ideas, James. It has been long enough now that people are forgetting the horror of those dry years and looking back to them as a time of possibility. These *people* don't seem to recall the dangerous implications of attempting to ban alcohol, for one can never stop its flow completely. After all, things naturally ferment. Sorry, I seem to be getting carried away." D took another sip from his golden glass. "But people are forgetting that the illegal alcohol that was then manufactured in the aftermath became much less safe to drink, as it very well might have been adulterated by the illicit production process. And also with our beloved alcohol now harder to obtain, people began turning to other substances that they wouldn't normally bother with if alcohol had been freely available. These are *both* consequences that concern our Service, Double-O Double-O. As well as this newly resurrected talk of 'cleaning up society'. What do you put on cuts and wounds, I ask you? In all seriousness, do you know how many people a year ingest rubbing alcohol if the real stuff isn't available? Oh wait, there I go again," D's rampage turning to laughter at his final comment. He sat for a moment reflecting and then declared, "No, it would be better if Prohibition had never existed at all."

"Sir?" James Vagabond hoped that this would be enough prompting. He did not want to appear stupid but he still had no clue what his superior could be getting at. Agitated, he fished out another Fumetti butt and lit it. He looked over at D who had now turned his seat a little and sat staring out the window into the dismal alleyway beyond, drumming an increasingly annoying rhythm on his golden pint glass. Vagabond took a beer out of his coat pocket, held it in his lap, and coughed as he extinguished the short cigarette butt after only two drags in the ashtray on the desk. It had hardly been worth lighting at all. Noisily he rummaged through the bowl choosing a more substantial smoke.

D showed no sign of returning to the matter at hand just yet. James continued to sit as he knew he must, puzzled and thirsty, D's incessant tapping putting him in mind of his Amsterdam messenger's flautist-phase. Two more painful minutes went by until D once again turned his head in Vagabond's direction, and nodding towards the unopened beer in James' lap, said, "Yes, of course, go ahead, Double-O Double-O." James appreciatively opened the can he would never have dared crack without D's permission.

"Where was I?" D asked as he scanned the bowl for a suitable smoke, sounding as if he didn't particularly care where he had in fact been. No matter how many times James had been through this routine of D drifting off in the middle of something important, these moments still never failed to unsettle him a great deal. "Oh yes," D remarked as he pulled out a surprisingly lengthy cigarette end, "it would be best if

Prohibition had never happened at all. And I think we've found a way to make that happen."

James bolted upright in his chair. He thought the old man might finally have lost it this time.

D continued, "A few weeks ago a certain professor made contact with our man 20/20. Lovely chap, still loves to dress up as a blind man... But anyway this professor, Professor Welles he calls himself, claims to have invented a time machine. We think this fellow might be German or Eastern European, but we haven't got any sort of background on him yet - we're working on it. He could just be drunk all the time. At least this was 20/20's impressions judging by the way this chap spoke. Remind me to tell you about 20's new recipe for, wait, what was it now? A Caligula's Horse? Anyway, a fantastic cocktail. Now our investigations into the credibility of the time machine seem to check out OK. The trouble is this Welles fellow has also offered it to the Americans, the White Russians, O.U.Z.O., the reigning beer..." (they paused for a moment, eyes to the sky, drooling at the possibility) "...agencies, W.I.N.O., and most likely the rest of them, all of whom would have a vested interest in using the thing."

James Vagabond rubbed his face with both hands, the beer can still clenched in his right. He was having trouble processing this information, let alone its implications. His mind searched for any complete question he could formulate out of the mass of confusion swirling around his brain. After a moment he ventured, "But sir, doesn't anyone want to use the machine for something non-alcohol related?"

"No," came the immediate response. D took a deep breath. "Welles is apparently a big-time drinker. He chose to offer his invention to the alcohol companies first and everyone has been on their honour about not letting the information slip. The bidding is getting quite high; we've heard reports of rivals offering lifetime supplies, multiple liver transplants guaranteed..."

"Multiple, sir?"

"Yes, that's correct, Double-O Double-O," D looked at him sternly. "In case following the first one he chooses to keep drinking and something goes wrong after that. That makes sense. He wants to be assured of drinking forever. Would have made a good agent."

"Sorry, sir. Of course." James Vagabond lowered his eyes in deference. "So have we made an offer yet?"

"That is where you come in, James," D choosing to use Vagabond's name to soften the former rebuke. "The first part of your assignment. And this is an order." D smiled. "The good professor is staying in Notting Hill Gate, where he believes our Service is located. It's obvious he can't quite figure out how we operate. A good thing. He spends most of his time at a bar where they serve a wide variety of absinthe drinks." D reached down, opened a drawer to his right, and threw an envelope onto the desk. "This is our bid. You are to take it to him tomorrow. And I do not have to remind you it is for his eyes only, not yours." D smiled again. This was common procedure; large quantities of alcohol, even if only in written form, often provoked jealousy or inspired mad, dangerous acts to obtain the booze for oneself.

James took the envelope and put it next to the beer in his coat pocket where he would be sure not to forget it. He thought for a moment and then asked, "Do we know what the others might be planning to use the time machine for, sir?"

"Vaguely. And it all seems to centre on Prohibition. Our sources tell us there is an American export company that wants to make sure Prohibition stays intact, that it was never repealed. But with a twist. They've had the idea that alcohol should still be allowed to be manufactured inside the United States for export, but it will be illegal to consume it - those bastards - therefore none could be imported. This will cut deep into their competitors' profits. We believe they would go back to the beginning of the movement and try to set everything up from there and then stay on to make sure it doesn't end. Now if you'll excuse me, Double-O Double-O, I think it's time for a nap. Would you please send Miss Glassbottle in on your way out? Deliver the envelope and if all goes well I'll be seeing you again shortly."

James Vagabond got up and strolled back to the secret passageway from which he had come. D watched his receding figure, the man who was technically known as just Double-O, but everyone had celebrated so much the day he received his number, they had all been seeing two of everything. Only Miss Glassbottle realised the mistake, a few days later, but she kept her mouth shut; by then she had already grown rather fond of the appellation.

3 – The Absinthe-Minded Professor

James Vagabond walked slowly on through the heavy night down Camden High Street, fingering the sticky envelope in his coat pocket with a sweaty hand. Amongst other things, he was trying to decide at which trash bin behind which restaurant he should have dinner. He paused in front of Camden Town tube station, considering the possibilities if he were to turn up Kentish Town Road. Stopping here, mulling over what he might find in that direction and if he would like to eat it out of a skip, he took a beer out of his pocket, the one that held the fateful envelope. No sooner had he cracked open the can and poured half its contents down his throat than he was accosted by a shadowy figure dressed much like himself, although he could not determine its gender via its voice or his own eyes.

"Gimme summa that!" the figure roared, grabbing at the container in James' hand. After a few attempts resulting in the character finally, with flailing limbs, latching onto the beer can as well, James relented, and whoever it was scampered away victorious. James shrugged his shoulders and opted to continue down Camden High Street. This was unlike him, something was wrong. D's words – 'The first part of your assignment' echoed over and over again in Vagabond's wet-walled mind.

James Vagabond was exhausted. Why had he been recalled from Amsterdam for the simple task of delivering an envelope? Was there some danger he was unaware of? Something D wasn't telling him? Why not 20/20 if D was so fond of him? Maybe that was precisely why. Rumours abounded about the two of them, D and 20/20, but nothing had ever been proven. D always spoke, as he had earlier this evening, extremely highly of that spectacular agent. James Vagabond never put much stock in the talk he heard on the streets about the two Servicemen he respected so. Vagabond always assumed the youthful 20/20 reminded the ageing D of himself in years past, and that D was trying to recapture some of the glory of his early life in the Service, when he was actually out there making it happen. There was not much glamour in being the anonymous mastermind who controlled everything behind the scenes - a post it was commonly believed 20/20 would be taking over someday. D would often wax nostalgic in his drunker moments, or at least what seemed like them, for there was the theory that the D stood for Detox and the man never actually touched a drop of alcohol anymore, was in fact still Drying Out (another possibility) after years of unheard-of alcohol abuse, and this was why his brain was able to operate on such a grander scale than any other member of the Service or, perhaps, the world. James Vagabond himself suspected the D was short for Drunk but there were other conjectures too – Drinker, Dipsomaniac, Dennis...

James looked up and realised he was approaching Mornington Crescent and therefore his eating options would begin to dwindle from then on out. Turning around, he focused more on deciding where to dine - if he were lucky the first wave of dinner trash might just have been thrown out and there was always the chance he'd find some leftover lunch that no one had gotten to yet.

After a minute he hurried behind one of his favourite cafés in North London. The one beer left on his person would not usually be enough to get to sleep on, but today had been exhausting - traveling through four countries, those funny ladies on the train, and a good amount of walking and thinking. He opened the trash bin lid, flipping it one hundred and eighty degrees so that it hung off its hinges on the other side. James was not disappointed. In plain view was a half-eaten mozzarella, basil, and tomato baguette perched on top of the heap of garbage. Nearby were swirls of loose spaghetti in cream sauce. He hoped the black bits dotted about them were pepper and not coffee grinds, a taste and texture you get used to but are always surprised by. He scooped the pasta onto the end of sandwich and shoveled it all into his eager mouth. His next find was a spinach pie that someone had stubbed a Grate out in. He removed the bent cigarette but unfortunately it wasn't salvageable; a beverage, non-alcoholic his senses immediately told him, had been poured over it at some point. James put his thumb into the hole where the Grate had been and tore off the pie around it with his other hand. Not bad, even if it was ginger ale-flavoured. There were other unidentifiable scraps of sandwiches lying about. The few that had discarded tissues sticking to them he chose to toss to the side. He paused to sip his beer for a second; satisfied with his meal. And now for dessert. After much digging James finally pieced together a handful of various mushy chocolate something-or-others. He scoured the ground for a smoke, which would be a nice final touch, but as the light was poor in the alleyway he came up empty handed. Finishing his beer, he tossed the can into the refuse and climbed in after it. Jumping over the pile of food from which he had just eaten, James settled into the shadowy trash on the other side, closing the lid over him. With all D's new information still racing through his mind, he drifted off to sleep.

The agency James Vagabond worked for was commonly referred to as DRINKS, although this was not an acronym. Plenty of times, late at night, if a few Servicemen were drinking together at a bar, down by the river, or in an alleyway somewhere it would be suggested that these letters *should* stand for something and lists would be compiled but never completed. Proposals would begin "Drunken Royal Intelligence...." or "Defense Retainers of Inebriated National..." Often the following exchange was heard - "International Network..." "Wait, you forgot the first two." And then whoever put forth the 'I' and 'N' would inevitably get stuck thinking up something for the letter 'D'. There was always 'Service' waiting at the end but it seemed impossible for anyone to get past 'K', and it always took an especially long time to arrive there, even if incongruous ideas such as "Duty Raki Igloo News Klub" and "Dozen Rooms I Now Know" were allowed to proceed that far. James recognised something in "Delicately Romantic Inverted Nights' Knights" but knew it didn't fully give an accurate account of what they were in business for.

DRINKS was referred to, derogatorily, as 'the Slurvice' by the opposing operations that kept the drug traffic going. These were mostly in charge of narcotics. There was no marijuana agency. Smokers of that drug could not be bothered to organise such a thing. The system governing the use of hallucinogenics was too far out there for anyone not directly affected by those substances to understand. Besides, hallucinogens didn't present much of a problem to the other

Services of the world. Those under the influence of LSD or psychedelic mushrooms had been known to ingest vast quantities of almost anything during the course of their trip. The Angels ran their dust and animal tranquiliser racket but they were more of a specialty case, there was never much trouble in that area. It was the narcotics agencies, the protectorates of cocaine and opiates, who posed the greatest threat to DRINKS. The cold, clear-headed thinking of those who did not indulge in the medium they worked in scoffed at the sloppy operations of DRINKS and its international counterparts. P.O.P.P.Y. and C.O.C.A. were the best-known narcotics agencies, and while there certainly must be others, it was widely believed that even these were fronts for something much bigger. Although nominally enemies, the opium and cocaine forces often worked together to achieve their common goals and DRINKS agents had run up against them the world over – international conferences, dark shipyards, university campuses – without being able to penetrate their setup very far at all.

James Vagabond awoke to the distant sound of drumming, stomping, and chanting. At first he thought it was the tribal ritual of his hangover but he soon realised this would be unjustified; he hadn't had much to drink at all last night. Still, his body and mind felt strange and after a minute he recognised this as the after-effects of travel, no doubt including learning of the mindwrenching possibility of that through time, and not his alcohol intake, whatever it had been. He had stopped counting the daily totals years ago. James perceived that the noises he continued to hear were not emanating from within but coming from somewhere outside the trash bin. 'Great,' he thought, 'the revolution has come and we're all done for. Whatever it is these people believe in there is sure to be a lot of broken bottles and wasted liquor in the riots.' He threw his head back into the pile of rubbish in disgust. The impact of his skull caused something to ooze out from under him. Clenching his eyes shut, James then laughed, realising these were his morning thoughts more often than not, regardless of the severity of any hangover. Best to be up and on his way. He had important and immediate business to attend to. Standing, he brushed himself off as best he could, climbed out of the bin, and set off back down Camden High Street towards Euston Station.

Two minutes into his walk he became conscious of the fact that the only concrete information he had been given was to deliver an envelope to a professor at a bar in Notting Hill Gate today. The envelope! James thrust his hand eagerly into his coat pocket, half-expecting to have lost it in the trash during the night. But luck was on his side. Reassuredly fingering the rectangular paper, he threw his hands up to the sky in thanks. Things like this were always happening. Ignoring the frightened looks of the passing pedestrians, he turned around and trudged back up the High Street from whence he had come. The sounds of 'the revolution' soon revealed themselves to be a united band of punks and hippies advertising a shoe sale somewhere. Presently arriving at the off-license next to headquarters he repeated the same procedure as the day before. Boss was a little puzzled at seeing Vagabond again so soon but the vexed look crossing James' features prevented him from asking any questions.

Miss Glassbottle opened the door and James rushed past her, barely registering that the top three buttons of her blouse were undone. D stood busily tucking his shirt in next to her desk. "Double-O Double–O, the good professor accepted our offer so soon? That is good news. Now let's get down to business. If you see yourself into my office, I'll be with you in a few minutes," D spat out in quick breaths.

"No, sir. He hasn't accepted yet. I was on my way to meet him when I realised that I didn't know my exact destination, nor whom I should be looking for were I to arrive there."

D put his hand to his forehead and chuckled softly. Things like this were also always happening. He went into his office for a moment and came back with a small photograph, holding it up to James. "Professor Welles." D then bent to the desk and scribbled something on the back of the print. "You should find him here just about now, for the remainder of the afternoon." James took the proffered picture and, glancing at it quickly, thrust it into his pocket next to the envelope. "Oh and James, here," D put four pound coins into James' palm, "Sorry for the trouble. Now get going so you don't miss him." D pushed Agent Double-O Double-O towards the doorway with one hand. James thought he heard him unzipping his trousers with the other. Hurrying down the stairway, James grabbed two more beers from the shelf, waved a friendly goodbye to Boss, and was on his way.

James downed his first beer of the day in almost one gulp and tossed the empty can to the side. He had understood that the four pounds D had put in his hand were to be used to take the Tube. D's way of making up for the mix-up and lost time. James wondered if he shouldn't just use the money to buy four cans of lager. He would most likely need more beer for his journey and there were certain secret subterranean passageways to avoid the ticket stalls, though not exactly efficient or easy to traverse. But by the time he reached Camden Town Station his conscience had won out and he obediently paid his fare and headed down the escalator.

James Vagabond boarded a not-too-crowded train heading towards Tottenham Court Road and found a seat in the corner. He opened his beer and peered about him. He could not remember exactly when he had last ridden the Tube but the trip stood out in his mind. Unusually drunk for whatever time of day it was, finding himself in an empty compartment, James had chosen to lie down on the floor. He wasn't sure how long he had been asleep but the next thing he knew there was a petite brunette straddling him, forcing her tongue down his throat. James tasted cheap wine on her panting breath and knew that she had been preparing for heading out on the town with her friends. You were trained to recognise such things in the Service. The distinct flavour of a date that hadn't gone particularly well or an enemy's intentions buried beneath the bourbon. The brunette had her way with him, rushing through the tunnels, and perfectly timed to bring her to her destination. She departed without a word and James went back to sleep, only leaving the car when later prodded by security. Such experiences were not uncommon on the Tube, he found. Now they were coming up on his stop and he ended his fond recollections to change to the Central Line.

Walking out into the fresh air at Notting Hill Gate, the first thing James did was to scour the ground for cigarettes. He found a good-sized Ifandor butt fairly quickly and looked about him for a means to light it. From out of nowhere, a youngish-looking blonde with a marvelous bust, only slightly covered by an extremely low-cut fawn dress, produced a lighter in front of James' face. He continued his downward gaze as he bent to light the cigarette and approved of her thin rhinestone belt and tan thigh-high boots. She took out a pack of Chestertons and held it open against her right breast as if one of the offered filters were an extension of her nipple. "Have another," she smiled, "for afterwards." She licked her lips as he took the cigarette, which she had positioned so he could not grasp it without touching her bosom.

"Walk me to Marble Archway, handsome," she ventured in what sounded vaguely like an American accent. James Vagabond was immediately put on his guard. As much as he would love to smoke that Chesterton with her 'afterwards', his mind returned to his duties, which had been mixed up enough today already. Even if she wasn't an American secret agent, or more likely another organisation's spy posing as an American visiting London, he had a job to do, and would have to refuse.

"I'm sorry, I must be on my way. There's no timmmme…" He coughed to stop the vibrations of that 'm', catching himself on the verge of adding 'machine'. She pouted and walked away without a word. Unfortunately the girl was heading in the direction that James now had to go in. He paused for a few minutes, smoking that titillating cigarette, and then was on his way. She was still in his sights for another minute before turning into a building James knew quite well. It was where the weekly support group convened for people whose favourite drinks have been taken off the market. The last time James had attended was when his Meister Brau import connection suddenly dried up. Ah, Meister Brau – so cheap, so tasty, so divine! The meetings had helped although they often made him rather sad, all those broken hearts who still, after ten, fifteen years couldn't get over their loss. But now, as he did then, James pulled himself together and moved on. He had business to attend to.

James checked the photograph once again in the fading daylight as he descended the stone stairs to the room where, with any luck, Professor Welles would be waiting for him. The place was relatively empty and as he walked up to the bar surveying the scene the heavily fake-tanned girl behind the counter slid a bottle of lager over to him, lifted her sunglasses with her right hand, and winked. Maybe D had tipped her off or perhaps she just fancied James; either way James was satisfied that he was drinking for free. He noticed a solitary figure over in a corner booth reading a periodical and consulted the photograph one last time. Bottle glasses, shabby suit, wiry grey hair, goatee, this was Welles alright. As James moved closer he noticed that the good professor was reading *CheMistress* magazine but Welles spotted Vagabond before James could get a good look at what the girl on the cover was doing with the test tubes. The professor casually slid *CheMistress* back into a plain brown bag that was already bulging with other, probably similar, reading material.

"Ah, Meister Vadge-a-bund," Welles stood and held out his hand, "sooo vairy goot to meetchoo."

James shook the offered hand. "Yes, good to meet you too, Professor." 20/20 was right, James thought. I have no idea where this man is from but he is obviously lashed. James eyed the table where they now sat and counted 11 empty glasses pushed towards the absinthe poster on the wall. The professor's already bulging eyes seemed to stretch out even further as he now brought a glass of green, pungent liquid to his full red lips.

"Half a cigarette," he offered, which James gladly took, "and I belief you half zumting for me?"

James reached into his coat pocket and tossed the envelope onto the table. He was glad the professor had gotten right down to business. James was always pleasantly surprised when people did. In a perfect world he would be able to head back to Camden Town now but he knew how important this was to D, and to the Service, so it was imperative he stay and make sure Welles was comfortable. The professor opened the envelope, eyed its contents quickly and stuffed it into his breast pocket.

"Excel-lensssssce," he enthused. "Excel-lensssssce." And then they sat in silence for quite some time. The professor didn't seem to mind so James relaxed. The girl behind the bar continued to bring them free drink after free drink, winking at James every time, often accompanied by more suggestive movements using cherries, miniature umbrellas, ice, and other unasked-for accoutrements. James couldn't tell if the professor observed this or not; his companion just sat casually rocking back and forth in his seat, smiling the smile of the insane, and drinking at a rapid pace. James wondered if the professor would notice if he were to get up from the table and take the barmaid behind the door marked 'Staff Only'. His fantasies were cut short by an eerie premonitory vision of looking up and seeing the professor watching them, perhaps taking notes or even photographs. James shuddered and quickly erased the mental picture from his mind.

"So you vill bee won going back to time, yes?" the professor asked after about an hour, nodding his head frantically as if in approval.

James gulped, swallowing like he had never swallowed before, even when risking the most dangerous cocktails he'd had to quaff or relishing the most delicious of secret brews. 'The first part of your assignment'...so that must mean if this Professor Welles was indeed accepting the Service's offer, then James would be the one carrying out the mission, the one going back in time. This was insane! Nerves fluttered his fingers on his seat, drumming a rhythm in distant echo of an infuriating flute. Madness since the very beginning, since that crazed tramp in Amsterdam had given him the message to report home to duty. James drank to steady himself, the whole of his being concentrating on the liquid calm gliding down his throat.

"Yes, I think so. I think it will be me," trying to sound positive, keeping the fear out of his voice.

"Oh, you vill luv," the professor smiled, "tis truly vumberfull, like being drunk," he raised his glass. And then in perfect English, "That is actually how I stumbled across it."

James didn't know the appropriate response to someone hinting at how they discovered time travel so he raised his glass, smiled, and took a long gulp. This seemed to satisfy the professor. After another hour or so of silence and many further free drinks the professor stood up, took his bag, and asked, "So vere are you brinking me now?"

As the two trudged their way up Brewer St., James remained unenthusiastic about taking Professor Welles out for the evening. He had been hoping against hope that this would not be required. He had so much else on his mind. James was surprised that the professor could still walk after all he had consumed and normally this would have made James respect him a great deal, but there was something strange about the man that James didn't trust, something he couldn't quite put his finger on. Clutching his bag to him, the professor smiled, and with a twinkle in his eye and much sentimentality in his voice, said, "Ah, back en Soho."

Entering a doorway marked 'Haircuts', the professor had turned quickly with James as if he had known exactly where they were headed, and this worried James for an instant. But in the next moment the professor was a crumpled mess on the floor, protectively clasping his magazines to his chest, and as James helped him up, he considered that perhaps the good professor had simply, finally, fallen down. They proceeded to the back, down a creaking stairway, and then up another one. The doorman nodded to James, motioning for him and the professor to go through. As they were being shown to a seat by a thin brunette, naked except for six-inch gold heels, James whispered to the professor, "Remember, you are not to give any of the girls money. It is all taken care of."

The professor smiled, sitting back with half-closed eyes.

"Two octo-voddies, please. Double D." James gave their order to a passing waitress, wearing only a sky blue bowtie.

The room the two gentlemen now found themselves in was the Service-funded strip club, Off The Rocks. It had seemed the logical place to show the professor a good time, a much better choice than the Brew-Ha-Ha, the Service comedy club. The drinks came in bra-cup sizes – A for shots, C for pints, but mostly the men drank DD-sized lagers, or the eight-way vodka concoction James Vagabond had just ordered. The audience was not allowed to give money to the strippers because the girls did not want to be constantly pawed by filthy hands. This hadn't always been the case; a few years ago there was a delousing station at the entranceway but the cost of disinfecting so many people at the door became too great and it also had a tendency to ruin an agent's cover. The Service decided that the most economical way of doing things was to pay the ladies a higher flat fee. Of course, most of the strippers were agents as well. After their second round of octo-voddies James looked over and noticed that the professor was fast asleep in his chair. Head hung back, drool dripping out of the corners of his mouth, Welles was even snoring lightly. James congratulated himself on a job well done. Recalling last night's spinach pie, he ordered a Stutter (gin, ginger ale) and settled back into his chair. He knew it would not be a problem for them to spend the rest of the night right there at their table.

"This is a dangerous operation, Double-O Double-O," D was saying, "particularly since you won't have any alcohol with you during your journey or upon arrival. The Professor says the procedure causes it to evaporate." Even with all his years of experience, D still could not suppress a shudder at his last statement.

James Vagabond had awoken early in his seat at the club. Professor Welles was nowhere in sight so James headed back towards Camden to make his report to D. He then spent the rest of the afternoon learning what he could about the American period of Prohibition. He was very thankful for the Internet - the books at the Service library, along with a good deal of files in the Records

Department, were constantly being misplaced. It was official; he would be the one going back in time. He now stood in D's office going over the final details.

"What about the historical implications of altering the course of time, sir?"

"Don't you go worrying about those, Double-O Double-O. You have enough to think about as it is. But I assure you we have people working on that end of it."

"And how am I supposed to wrap this thing up?"

"I don't know, Double-O Double-O. You'll have to figure that out for yourself once you get there. Unfortunately we have no contacts or any inside information where you're going."

Miss Glassbottle opened the door and peered around the corner seductively, immediately shutting it again with a reddening look of embarrassment. D stood up and quickly shook James' hand, "Good luck, Double-O Double-O."

4 – Ocean Bin Liners

In the plush burgundy interior of a black cab speeding smoothly towards Southampton, James Vagabond took another unlabelled lager from the fridge in front of him. Ernst, one of the men the Service employed on their sober schedule, precisely for such purposes, was driving. When this system had been instated (long gone were the days when agents were allowed to drive themselves, as were the cars that contained a fully-stocked bar in place of a passenger seat), James had been adamantly against the idea. He didn't trust anyone who didn't drink, and barely trusted most people when they were sober. It had taken some time for D to calm down an irate James Vagabond and make him understand that these men did in fact imbibe, just not on the job. James now lit a cigarette and cracked open the window slightly. It takes all types to make a world, he mused. After James had finally grasped D's reasoning, he made it a point to take every single one of these 'sobers' to Off The Rocks to see what they were made of. Most passed the test; although there were a few drivers that James requested only be used in case of an emergency. James had been suitably impressed with Ernst's drinking abilities, not least by the fact that Ernst would keep his cigarette between his lips whilst throwing back a shot. In an effort to make James as comfortable as possible before his historic mission, D had specifically bestowed upon Ernst the job of taking James to the ship.

As the time machine only traveled through time and not space, Steven Kingston, head of Station RUM, was in charge of transporting the contraption to Florida. Keeping man and means separate for safety's sake, once in Southampton James was to be stowed away on the Queen Bea, setting sail for America that afternoon. West Indian Pale Alex, undercover as a barkeeper on board, would ensure the trans-Atlantic crossing went smoothly. Being perched above seemingly infinite non-alcoholic liquid, and salty at that, was a nightmare common to all agents, haunting their dreams to the point of DRINKS instituting reconditioning countermeasures. It was now compulsory for an operative to spend 24 hours every other year aboard CARAFT, the Service cruiser. A harrowing experience, but also an exercise to encourage positive thinking. Conquering one's fears would bring about the cordial sensation of floating and a full appreciation of the pleasures in being adrift on a vessel stocked, as boats often were, with a full bar five times over. Though even now with such a course fresh in his memory, James had tried his best to be put on a plane to Milwaukee. He had heard rumours that in that sudsy city the streets were paved with gold and you could take that gold and buy beer with it. But flying - with its mocking miniature bottles - was frowned upon by the Service. Coming up on the port now, James began to fill his pockets with beer from the cab's refrigerator.

"Hello, old friend," Pale Alex greeted James warmly, "Come along, we must hurry." Moving quickly along the quayside, they soon arrived at a large wooden crate, drilled-in air holes visible to James' discerning eye. They raced through standard stowaway procedure and James found there was enough room to make himself comfortable. Taking off his jacket, he rolled it into a pillow and settled in for a nap. Pale Alex gave the box a departing thump. Soon the swaying motion of the crate being loaded on board lulled James off to sleep.

When he awoke it was completely dark and James instinctively reached inside his coat for a beer. Banging his head as he sat up to drink it, he more practically now pulled out the cigarette lighter he had taken from the cab. With visions of towers of tequila and Tia Maria dancing through his aching cranium, he flicked the flame to see just what goodies he was traveling with.

"Dammit" he swore out loud. "Can't these people get anything right?" He moved the lighter past the boxes of orange juice hoping against hope that they might have stored some gin in there too. But no, row upon row of apple, cranberry, grapefruit. Mixers! Unbelievable! James was having none of it. His thirst greatly aggravated, he pulled out the specially made 2-gallon bottle of vodka that was his sole luggage for the journey. He wouldn't be putting any of the foolish nectar surrounding him into it either; he had a good mind to burn the lot of it, if only it would burn.

Soon James noticed streams of light cascading into the crate and heard a faint knocking at his side before the lid was hoisted off. Pale Alex beamed down at him. "I see you're making yourself at home," nodding towards the half-empty bottle James was holding. During the first third of the bottle James was determined to tear into Pale Alex when he next saw him about the inadequacy of the situation. He knew there must be plenty of crates of alcohol on board, nearby even, but now, having drunk as much as he had, James Vagabond was more of the mind that this was just another charming little example of the way his Service operated. He belched in response, hoping it conveyed these thoughts and emotions to his friend.

"I brought you some food," offered Pale Alex, producing a plate. "I didn't have much time, just enough to slide the remains of a deserted table on here. But it's from the Queen's Grille." Pale Alex sounded almost apologetic. But James was delighted; he could already tell from the teeth marks in the Lobster Thermidor and scraps of Châteaubriand that this was a feast fit for a king. "I've got to skedaddle, working at the Lido Bar in ten minutes. I'll try and sneak you another bottle later on, if you'll need it."

James gave him a withering look.

"Sorry, Double-0 Double-0. I'll leave the lid loose in case you want to walk around later. But please, be careful."

James watched Pale Alex depart, pouring the multi-coloured mess on his plate straight down his throat, tasting vaguely of honey, blissfully ignoring the half-eaten bits that had obviously been chewed and spat back out again.

James finished his bottle and threw it into the boxes of tomato juice. "Bloody mixer!" he sneered. He was growing restless, the food and vodka giving him energy. It was time to stretch his legs, see where they stored the alcohol if Pale Alex was going to take his jolly time in bringing him more. He carelessly knocked the lid off the top and stood up. The clock in front of him read 2:14. Aha! Everything would be closed by now and he could walk around the decks unnoticed, looking for those metal buckets of sand people discarded their cigarettes in, or even an ashtray. He vaulted out of the crate, landing on one foot, and promptly fell over, rolling into a pole beside him. 'Haven't got my sea legs yet,' he reasoned. Hobbling to the doorway, James saw the coast was clear and cautiously began to make his way to the deck above. With any luck the crew would not have cleared away the half-emptied glasses from the tables surrounding the pool.

The night sea air hit him like an empty can as he stumbled outside and was forced to grab hold of the railing. Slowly finding his bearings, he staggered towards the swimming area. No one was about, but the tables had already been cleaned dry and no discarded cigarettes were to be seen anywhere. He carefully made his way to the opposite end of the deck but peeking around the wall, he slipped, grabbing hold of the railing with a thud. The woman sitting on the deck chair in the shadows jolted up in alarm, exclaiming "Oh!" in a voice more delighted than startled.

"Please, come join me! Would you like a cigarette?"

James accepted graciously, eyeing this curious female. Her breast-length black hair blew furiously in the wind, a string of pearls dancing about her neck, and her spaghetti-strapped evening gown, the shade of the sky beyond, gladly clung on for dear life to those curves. James sensed there was no underwear underneath. Circling her right wrist was a gold clasp, shimmering into view as her hand reached for the champagne under her chair. No glass in sight, she swigged it straight from the source, James thinking 'This is my type of woman.' But in the next second with a laugh she threw the bottle overboard and James felt something akin to heartache.

"I'm sorry," she apologised seeing the look in James' eye. "That was the last of it. But there's more in my room. C'mon," she took his hand, still greasy from wiping his mouth after dinner. "It's right downstairs."

The rocking of the ship ushered a complicated, ungraceful procession – limbs locking, falling over and into each other, prolonged groping as much for ballast as pure carnality – to her awaiting cabin. The vixen probed James' pockets for her keys until, unable to contain themselves, she remembered they were in her purse. Bursting into the room, the champagne bottle was found and at points even incorporated into the wild drunken gymnastics continuing for another three-quarters of an hour. After a symphonic climax coinciding with the popping of the cork, she rolled off James still panting and purring. Mouths open, James poured the bottle over their exhausted faces. Splashing and slurping and licking the drips from each other's lips, they soon fell contentedly asleep.

Waking late the next afternoon, they were at it again before both had fully regained consciousness. Repeating their performance from the early hours, this session even more acrobatic, and vocal on her part. Considering the state of filth he constantly lived in, James usually felt 'dirty talk' to be along the lines of social realism in art, lacking imagination. But the inventiveness of this paramour was truly inspired –"that's the tap you've been thirsting for", "smash me like a hollow barrel" - spurring him on to total blackout at the ultimate moment. This was just as well, as the ensuing state of complete physical and mental relaxation prepared him for the fact that there wasn't any alcohol left in the room. Breathing deeply and focusing on the problem, James soon remembered that Pale Alex would have left another bottle in his crate. Now how to get it without offending the lady…

His thoughts were interrupted by the rustling of pillows. "Oh, I'm sorry, my name is Venus, Venus Maher."

"That's a lovely name, Venus," and it started all over again.

When they had quite finished, Venus produced a pack of Jupiters from a bedside drawer and lit one for each of them. "And you are?"

"Vagabond. James Vagabond," he replied as he inhaled luxuriously.

"Vagabond, hmmm. That's an interesting name, where does it come from?"

James wrinkled his forehead. "Well, my father was a Vagabond," he responded vaguely and Venus was too well-mannered to inquire any further. Instead she stubbed out her cigarette in the nightstand ashtray, got up, and moved towards the bathroom. James registered the half-smoked Jupiter for later. Good, he observed. His senses were getting themselves in shape for his upcoming mission.

Venus appeared again, curling herself around the bathroom door. "Come shower with me, James."

A most difficult dilemma. Impossible to refuse the invitation, but the effects of accepting such were devastating to one's whole appearance, and for quite some time. It had taken James months to arrive at his present look, his last bath was a distant dispiriting memory, and now his carefully cultivated image would be destroyed in minutes. James thought of his mission, but knew it was hopeless. He consoled himself with the fact that at least by the time he arrived in Florida he would be well on his way back to normal. In fact it was imperative to dirty himself up again by Florida or else they wouldn't recognise him. Standing up, reconciling himself to obeying Venus' orders, he recalled all those times in London when after sleeping with some owner of a multi-national corporation or other, he would be lured into a shower and then forced, out of honour, to hide in the filthiest alleys for days on end until he regained some of his former 'radiance'.

"Come now, James," Venus took his hand and pulled him under the hot streaming water. He choked back the urge to vomit after watching the departing flows of black, grey, and brown swirl down the drain. Venus seemed not to notice as she lathered his thick beard with soft, massaging hands. "I'll shave yours if you shave mine," she offered provocatively. But here was where James drew the line. Springing moodily from the shower, Venus caught James' arm just in time and settled for cleaning his beard instead. To Venus' delighted amusement she collected in her hand several strands of spinach, flecks of lobster and scraps of steak, one bottle cap after another (convenient for meeting other agents), a few small pieces of paper bearing women's telephone numbers, and in one particular pull a bird feather.

Afterwards, she hopped out of the shower, threw a towel around herself, and called back to James as she stepped into the bedroom, "Hurry up, I'll put you in some of my husband's clothes and then we'll go for a drink."

James froze in shock well before she got to the word 'drink'. Husband? What had he gotten himself into? Cavorting so carelessly around her cabin...and where was her husband now? Off with some other woman while she was free to seduce James with promises of drink? And then let James wear his clothes? If all this was acceptable, would this mean that at some point during the cruise James would have to oblige the two of them together for their hospitality? He wasn't necessarily opposed to the idea, but exploring his sexuality might not be the best course of action right now. He needed to keep his head clear in order to focus on going back in time and then stopping Prohibition from ever happening. James started to gulp, coughing and spluttering out water in confusion and dismay. "So where is your husband now?" he ventured.

Venus poked her head back into the bathroom and looked in at him cringing in what must be the cold water. She shut off the tap. "He's in New York at a business conference. As soon as the ship pulls in, we're off to Moon Valley Canyon in Arizona to visit my sister. I packed an extra bag for him. Come take a look, pick out what you like." James breathed a heavy sigh of relief, quickly toweling himself off, hopeful that his appearance wasn't too damaged, and followed her towards the open suitcase. It took a second to register and he stopped dead in his tracks.

"New York?" Trying to keep the agitation out of his voice.

"Yes, handsome. New York. Our final destination."

James let forth an angry sigh. 'Typical. Just typical. The day this Service gets anything right, I'll drink a glass of unadulterated lemonade with a smile.' Careful not to let Venus see his consternation, he began enshrouding himself in unripped and non-stained gentlemen's evening dress, letting his subconscious mind solve the problem of how to get to Florida, where he was expected.

When James was fully clothed they went down to O'Shea's Lounge for aperitifs before heading in to the Bea Restaurant. Venus had dined alone at a table for two the previous night; no one thought twice when James Vagabond joined her this evening. Only the wine steward was slightly concerned at the rate an agitated James was ordering Chilean reds, vodka-infused German whites, and complex Blue Curaçao-based beverages, four at a time no less. Nominally it was two for the lady and two for James but when the glasses arrived, Venus drank one to James' three. Uneasy in such an environment and befuddled by the silverware, even such copious amounts of booze couldn't help steady James' hand to hold onto a fork for more than a few seconds at a time. Venus passed off James' clumsiness as a result of this rapid drinking pace.

"Really, James, you act as though you've never been in a restaurant before!" she laughed. Ordering a plethora of alcohol to be sent to the room, they quickly rushed back to Venus' cabin for dessert, sampling the menu on the stairs, then again in the corridor. The next two days passed in much the same manner until the penultimate night when so much rocking of the boat left Venus somewhat seasick. "But you go out, darling. Have a good time. Don't worry about me, I'll be okay."

"...and you mix it up in a used beer can? That's what gives it the flavour? Genius."

James Vagabond sat on the furthest but one stool at the rounded bar in the Golden Rose Lounge, regaling Pale Alex with the latest cocktail recipes on the street. His current tipple was a simple scotch on the rocks that had been, naturally, on the house, and naturally double. A television flickered silently behind the bar. On the Queen Bea, 'Arthur', the Dudley Moore film, seemed to play continuously on most of its channels. Pale Alex had been slightly concerned at not seeing James for the past three days. If it hadn't been for the fact that James was still picking up the daily whisky ration left for him, Pale Alex would've had to somehow alert D back in London that Vagabond had gone missing. Alex now listened, relieved and amused, as James recounted his time on board thus far. The two passed most of the evening in casual conversation and as Pale Alex busied himself washing the abundance of dirty glasses that had gathered in that time, Vagabond peered about the room. There were far less women about than only moments ago. James had felt their presence strongly as each beauty in turn would run their tongue slowly over the lemon peel or cherry in her drink, holding his gaze longingly for the duration. He also now noticed the growing clatter of the men, the pats on the back and unsure footing as they made their way to the previously unoccupied piano. Oh no, thought James, a song. Simultaneously, sloppily-played introductions, in the wrong keys no less, to Mötley Crüe's 'Home Sweet Home', Kiss' 'Beth', and Billy Joel's 'The Piano Man' began, the gathering oblivious to its cacophony. Voices grew louder, riding on violent undertones, as each vied for their song, or in one case 'Your Song', but a wondrous instant of synchronicity resolved everything as at least four hands and numerous voices burst into 'Hey Jude'.

James swirled the ice around in his glass hoping to conjure a way out. The ceaseless 'Na's' were growing in strength and number. James picked an unfiltered Nice Shot out of the ashtray watching the men swaying with raised arms, spilling each other's drinks. A sure sign you should cease whatever it is you're doing. Music is sacred but no Service in the world had yet figured out how to stop such scenes without simply shooting the place up. James regretted that he was traveling, out of necessity, unarmed. Why couldn't they be playing 'Born to Run' with its poignant 'Tramps like us' line? Or Nick Cave, Tom Waits, The Pogues, hell, even Chumbawamba. Now there was a song – the chap takes a drink, then another drink, and then probably another one... James sighed and picked up the half-full glass of whisky someone had left sitting next to him on the bar. Although he ethically disagreed with men abandoning their beverages for such, or any, activities, there was no reason why he shouldn't benefit from it. Downing the oak-aged elixir in one go, he signaled to Pale Alex for another, almost certain the recorded version of 'Hey Jude' had not gone on for this long.

Vagabond now grimaced as far too many men took the high 'Jude-Jude-Judy etcetera' vocal part. Looking up, he noted the last of the ladies leaving the lounge. His eyes followed their swaggers as the posterior posteriors disappeared in the darkened doorway. Seconds later two faint faces peered back around the corner and a pair of painted, bejeweled hands beckoned for Vagabond to come hither. Delightedly departing the dissonant drone, James raced down the bar polishing off the contents of every unattended glass, snatching a newly opened pack of Cellos left by the lemons.

James offered a smoke to each of the ladies in turn as they clasped and fondled his arms, escorting him to the swimming area. Every woman he had seen at The Golden Rose Lounge this evening – thirty-two, he was quick to count - was out on deck, presumably all the companions of the McCartney impersonators. Evening dresses lay loosely slung over sunbathing chairs and the bounty of black lingerie brought a smile to James' features. Like a sexy chess match, the white undergarments of the beauty queens in the pool now captured his attention. As his eager eyes scanned the night for more, his gaze soon settled on a group of dejected damsels, distressingly still fully dressed, sullenly smoking on the steps of the whirlpool.

"Why the pouty lips, ladies?"

"We wanted to go in the Jacuzzi," a luscious redhead looked up into James' eyes and, overcome by his magnetism, slid her body against his as she regained her feet. She paused, savouring the sliver of salt air between their lips. "But it's empty," she explained on tiptoe, her cleavage now obscuring James' view of anything else.

James took a deep breath and thought for a moment. He noticed out of the corner of his eye that the rest of the women were beginning to crowd in around him. His instincts kicked in, searching for an escape route and in doing so he spotted the pool bar.

"Give me one minute. I think I may be of some assistance." He ducked and darted his way out of the swarm of breasts, tongues, and hands being thrust at his person. If this was a trap, it was a damn good one. But fortune again seemed to be on his side. Slipping behind the bar, he tried the door to the refrigerator - unlocked! Working quickly he loaded up an impossible armful of champagne and sparkling wine bottles, running them, with all the urgency of the situation, over to a table beside the whirlpool. Dodging once again the female body parts strategically placed in his path, he rushed back for more and repeated the process a third time before stopping for calculations. James returned for one last load, noting that the bar refrigerator was now bordering on empty.

Lighting another cigarette and leaning against the stash, he smiled "Ladies, we're in luck!" James uncorked the first Jeroboam with due ceremony, pouring its contents into the awaiting Jacuzzi tub. He tossed the empty bottle into a nearby stack of towels as the women began removing the remainder of their clothes, dispersing them with wild abandon every which way about the deck. Diligently James filled the vessel with the assortment of pale bronze liquid, batting away eager hands attempting to pull him in before it was ready. Finally rolling the last bottle to the side, James gleefully dove in with the women hot on his heels. Now this was a bath he could enjoy!

James Vagabond awoke sometime the next morning to the sun burning his eyes and the sound of a Mariachi band. What revolution is this? But the lingering pleasures of the previous evening bubbled back to the surface of his mind, reinvigorating him, and he sat up to survey his surroundings. He was draped across a sunbathing chair, still on the same deck as last night's festivities. The bottles were gone and someone had, thankfully, placed a towel over his nether regions. His body felt as if it had been rolled naked through a sugar factory and then wrapped like a mummy. His senses were exhausted and frayed as if the nerve endings had all burst beyond repair, but his brain told him that he was very happy. He tried to recall what he could of the night before. It had all the sensual pleasure of the train ride home from Bruxelles but with the added bonus of that sensual pleasure taking place submerged in alcohol. And, he had almost forgotten, it had taken him away from a gaggle of drunken men attempting to sing a Beatles song. The Jacuzzi tub itself had been rather small compared to the amount of bodies wanting to use it, so the girls had naturally instituted a tag team system. James had once tagged himself out for a breather, finding sitting on the side of the tub watching the lapping waves of the maelstrom to be also quite exhilarating, but his absence was quickly noticed and he was just as speedily dragged back in again. James wasn't sure if the Jacuzzi had ever actually been turned on but what a whirlpool it had been.

A sexy shadow suddenly blocked the sun from James' eyes. Venus stood above him laughing, "And where have you been?" She pulled James up by the hand and as he began to detail the events of the night before, Venus, overcome with excitement, steamrolled him back to her room and forced James to demonstrate the highlights, forgetting all about the romantic lunch she had planned. Afterwards, the dried sweat now chafing his sugarcoated skin, James consented to one last shower. Their final night together was tearful in many ways. In the morning, James was relieved to learn that Venus had stored his Service clothes in a corner of her closet, and particularly pleased that she had not taken it upon herself to have them washed. "But please, keep these old rags," pointing to her husband's clothes. "He'll never notice they're missing, and they look so scrumptious on you."

At first James refused but then remembered he might need to be properly dressed if he planned on walking off the boat. As nothing had been arranged with Pale Alex, it looked as if this was going to be the best course of action. James removed his passport from a filthy boot and packed his old clothes into one of Venus' spare suitcases.

Then they made slow passionate love one last time until the call came to disembark.

As they approached the stairway above the exit gangplank, Venus let go of his hand. "You go ahead, darling, I can't risk letting my husband see me." She kissed him softly, whispering, "It was wonderful, James." Standing for a moment to brush the tears from her eyes, Venus then turned away, forever.

James Vagabond set foot in New York with the sweetest memories of those sex sea ladies swirling around his head, and a fondness for Venus swelling in his heart. It would be a few more minutes before he was ready to let go of them and turn his mind completely to his mission.

Lost in reverie, not paying careful enough attention to where he was going, James walked straight into a clean-shaven man of about his height and build. "Excuse me, sir!" The gentleman's annoyance quickly fading as he eyed James with approval. "You know, I have a jacket just like that."

James smiled and was quickly off.

5 – Closing Time

James Vagabond squinted into the lush noonday sun shimmering over New York Harbor. Now, on dry land, he felt more adrift than ever. Consulting a map, James found himself at least 1000 miles from where he needed to be, from where he had expected to be. He started walking, eyes scanning the horizon for the welcoming doors of a pub; in the bliss of his final days on board he had forgotten to stock his pockets with bottles. 'Must start getting in shape for this mission', he reprimanded himself. Once at the *bar* however, he realised he still wouldn't have any money and would have to rely on the kindness of strangers to pay for his drinks. Dressed in Mr. Maher's finery, no one would believe he was broke. Running to the nearest restroom, James changed back into his old rags, leaving suit and suitcase behind where he considered they belonged. He took a deep, noxious breath, feeling like himself again. Outside there was still no drinking establishment in sight but luckily the ground was covered in discarded cigarette butts. Picking up a handful, he lit one luxuriously, shuffling off in no particular direction.

Within minutes a yellow cab pulled up alongside of James and rolled its window down.

"Hey pal, are you James Vagabond?"

James stopped and squinted but said nothing. The driver continued, "It's okay, buddy, I'm a friend uh Ernie's." It took James a minute to realise this man might mean Ernst and softened the expression on his face to one of mild interest. "C'mon compadre, we ain't got all day. It's a free ride I'm offering you here!"

Hopping in the back, James was at first confused by the lack of a refrigerator. He felt around but could not find any hidden compartments where drinks might be stored. The cabbie barked, "You lookin' for sumthin', mister?"

James stopped fidgeting and inclined his head forward hopefully, "I was hoping to find a drink."

"Yeah, right," the man at the wheel scoffed, "got some water up here if you want?"

James ignored what he took to be an insult. He was not enjoying the ride so far, however free it was, and hoped to be out of the vehicle as soon as possible. "Where to, Mac?" asked the driver, half-turning in his seat.

Vagabond cleared his throat. "Sunset Beach, Florida, please."

"You're full of 'em today, eh, funny guy?"

Thinking quickly, James answered, "Anywhere on 7th Avenue is fine."

The cabbie shrugged, "Okay, J.V."

James reclined in his seat, uneasy about the situation. It was hard to believe this man could be a friend of Ernst. But chauffeurs, especially ones arranged speedily, were hardly ever let in on the bottlecap code. On the other hand, arriving in New York when he was supposed to be in Florida reeked of his Drunken Secret Service. He doubted this was enemy action. On 7th Avenue he knew an agent undercover as a pickle distributor who could hopefully help him out of this one.

"I don't know how you Brits can drink that warm beer…"

"That's it," James jumped. "You can let me off here."

"Have it your way, limelord." The cab swung to the curb and James hopped out as quickly as he could. He did not turn around to see the driver smiling in the rearview mirror.

Immediately James was witness to a scene that horrified him. An attractive policewoman in a blue uniform just the right side of tight was pouring a young man's forty-ounce malt liquor jug into the gutter. James thought about diving underneath for a quick sip or two, just to wash away the distaste of the cab ride, but an emerging fantasy of this law enforcement officer handcuffing him to a rare Speyside single malt bottle distracted him further. The woman was holding a driving license up to her eyes, viewing it skeptically, "And how old are you?"

"Twenty-three," the youth replied coolly.

"It says here that you are twenty-nine."

Flexing his bicep and jutting out his chest, the youngster put as much flirtation into his voice as he could muster. "And how old are you?" James Vagabond sped on, before the law could take notice of him.

Ah, Americans, James mused. He didn't quite know what to make of them. The USDS (United States Drinking Service, though often referred to as 'SUDS') was as diverse as the country itself. Each state and often city had its own agency, not to mention the fact that there was also a National Drinking League and American Drinking League. On James' last visit to the States, the far-right Puritan Drinking Party had been gaining power. Encouraging celibacy as most people didn't usually drink during the act of sex, they also, somewhat sensibly James considered, forbade mixers under any circumstances. A dying breed. But there was no doubting the American passion for drinking, their fervour when found in countries with laxer age limits, the warehouse-sized liquor stores, or just taking a quick look around any social event. Hell, the income tax arose to cover the cash lost by the government in alcohol duties when Prohibition was instated. This sobering thought brought James back to the full terror of his mission.

A tap on the shoulder interrupted Vagabond's reveries. Turning to see who it was, James noticed he was standing in front of Penn Station. A muscular man in overalls and sunglasses under a blue conductor's hat lowered a large bottle-shaped brown paper bag from his lips with his left hand. "Care for a sip, my man?" But before passing over the concealed container, his right hand shook and shocked James' as Vagabond registered the sweet relief of bottlecap pressing into palm. James drank much more than a sip, the agent continuing smoothly, "The name's K.C. Jones and I'll be handling your baggage this evening." Refreshed, James passed the bottle back to Mr. Jones, who after drinking deep again himself and discarding the now emptied bag, instructed, "Now if you'll care to follow me." The two set off carrying nothing but a slight buzz.

Loading James Vagabond onto the storage car of a train headed for Florida that evening, K.C. patted him on the back. "You're all set. Just stay in here and everything should be fine." James quickly clocked the twelve-pack of beer and two thinner bottle-shaped brown paper bags. He smiled. Sliding the door shut, K.C. called through, "Oh, and Miss Michel will be picking you up at the station. Bon voyage."

The door closed with a bang and James found himself surrounded by boxes and shadows. Lunging toward the beer, he settled into a comfortable corner. There was still some time to go before the train was due to leave. By his calculations, if he took a quick nap after this first beer, there would be provisions enough to get sufficiently drunk when he woke up later. He drifted off into a light sleep with the almost empty can clasped in his hand.

James Vagabond awoke after two hours, automatically finishing the beer he happened to still be holding. Rejuvenated after his rest, he eyed the stash of alcohol K.C. Jones had left for him, opening another can. Yes, this would do, he may have to pace himself, but it just might last the journey. Ten more beers to go after this one and then the two mystery bottles. He rubbed his hands together, wondering what they might be. Only one way to find out. Choosing to exercise the more appropriate sense of taste as opposed to sight, James greedily grabbed the first bottle and glugged down three quick gulps.

Strawberry Orange Vodka? How strange. Checking the label to confirm his guess, STRawberry orANGE Vodka was indeed what it said. Stranger still that this would be the first choice with which to supply him, even if rations had needed to be gathered in a hurry. The potation was pleasant enough, however, and as its level sank towards the bottom, James was even more curious about the second bottle. He soon regretted this. Utterly confounded, he swirled whatever this fluid was around his mouth, cascading it across his teeth and over his gums, finally forced to gargle and admit defeat. Sweet, tart, and gamey, but naming this dispiriting spirit was beyond his highly trained powers of recognition. Stunned and stumped, he could feel the question marks hovering over the dots of his taste buds. He tore off the brown paper covering. Kiwi Quail Schnapps? KIWI QUAIL SCHNAPPS???!!! A man was going back in time to stop Prohibition from ever happening and you give him Kiwi Quail Schnapps??? This was simply unbelievable. He swallowed bitterly and reluctantly, realising that this was all he had to drink for the duration of the ride.

James awoke face down in his own drool to the sound of the train slowing down. The last thing he remembered was throwing his arms up in victory as the last dregs of Kiwi Quail Schnapps slid down his throat, then falling into a pile of empty beer cans. Moving his head to rest on his other cheek, his mouth swiped through the pool of saliva, reliving the fowl taste again. The train had not been stopped a second when James cracked the door open, never more in need of fresh air and wishing to leave the ghost of the disorientating liquor behind him. The coast being clear, he jumped out and made his way towards the parking lot. The afternoon sun beat down heavily, steam rising from the asphalt, but James did not notice, his only concern was finding a proper drink as soon as humanly possible.

"Mr. Vagabond?"

"Miss Michel?" James could hardly believe it. He was actually in Florida. At least thcy got something, two things, right. The scant blue bottom that this knockout was wearing vied for his attention with her heaving breasts - one barely covered by a small patch of red and the other equally exposed in white. Her auburn hair blew in the light wind under a wide straw hat and she was tan down to her toes (his pleased pupils had moved back down again), all but one of which were ringed, wriggling back and forth in her sandals. But it was her warmth of spirit coupled with her abundant enthusiasm that truly captivated James. She held out her hand for Vagabond to shake, chills racing down his spine as her forefinger seductively slid the length of his palm, over the bottle cap pressed firmly into his heart line.

"That's me, Foxy J. Michel. My friends call me Foxy. And you," she was practically bouncing, "can call me anytime you like." She slid her arm through his, leading him to a waiting cream lime 1966 Lotus Elan HNK 999C. Foxy gave him a playful pat on the behind when he followed her to the door. "Other side, silly." Even this first slight parting was anguish as he noticed the steering wheel on the wrong side of the car, but his eyes soon settled on the salve of a cooler in the passenger seat. Before he could ask "Is this for me?" Foxy blew him a kiss and threw open the lid. "You must be so thirsty." A welcoming assortment of the best that American brewers had to offer bathed his features in a golden glow. As he cracked open the first, washing away the Kiwi Quail once and for all, James reflected that Foxy was the type of girl one could fall in love with, and hoped against hope there was room in the time machine for two.

Foxy sped on, pointing out some of the sights. "There's Sunset Beach, and Treasure Island. And there's the Rum Emporium, but to fully appreciate that palace would take more time than we've got. Unfortunately."

"So where are we going anyway, Foxy?"

"Well, we've scouted the area, going over the survey maps from the nineteen-teens, and moved the machine to Ted Williams' house...not the baseball player..." Catching James' look of confusion, she batted her eyelids at him and continued. "The house wasn't built until the 1940s. Before that the land was just brush and woods. You'll have to remember to hide the machine once you've arrived...there shouldn't be anyone around for miles, but you know, just in case."

Transfixed by her fingers caressing the gearshift, James' gaze slid to the patch of blue beyond. "Foxy," he took another sip of beer and turned towards her, "what does it look like?" He coughed nervously. "The machine."

"Oh, you'll see." Foxy smiled, hitting the accelerator. Keeping the cooler on his lap, James closed his eyes for the remainder of the ride.

"James, James. Wake up." James Vagabond blinked slowly awake, unsure if he was being shaken or given one of the most sensuous massages he'd ever experienced. He smiled up at Foxy from the passenger seat, well aware but not remarking upon the fact that her hands were underneath his shirt. "C'mon, I'll show you around. Ted Williams, we call him Bill," she smiled, "is in St. Petersburg, the other one, for the month. I've been watching the place, getting everything in order." Walking through the rear kitchen entrance, Foxy glided down the countertop, pouring James a double whiskey without pausing their procession. "And here it is, in here." She pushed open a door marked 'OUT OF ORDER' and James' mouth dropped in awe.

A telephone booth. Well, it would be, wouldn't it? Of the American variety too, silver paned, and sitting in a bathtub. He quickly shoved the glass of whiskey into his mouth to keep from expressing any doubts. Foxy had obviously worked very hard on this and it would break his heart to insult her. Beaming with pride, she climbed into the tub and opened the glass door of the booth.

"We thought it best to hide it here." James looked up, noting that the window was high enough that anyone looking in would not be able to see the machine. Foxy continued, "We couldn't have it upstairs because when you arrived back in time you'd have had a good twelve-foot drop to the ground." A look of deep concern momentarily tightened her brow. "Well, here's how it works. It's pretty easy." She smiled reassuringly. "Just dial in the date you want to go back to – day, then month...don't worry, that confused me at first too…then year – and when you're done with that, press the pound sign. So just let me know when you're ready, tiger."

James smiled, "As soon as I'm drunk enough, Foxy. As soon as I'm drunk enough."

"Right, let's go then!" She bounded out of the tub, pulling James through to the living room. James felt conflict tear at his very being. The agent in him wanted to go soon, to get on with his mission. And although fear was a failing he rarely tolerated, he recognised something of it in his wanting to get this time travel business over with. But Foxy had cast a spell over him that would be nearly impossible to break.

They spent the whole afternoon drinking together in the air-conditioned living room. Foxy suggested, and James quite agreed, that he did not want to risk sunstroke. She matched him shot for shot, beer for beer, and James was, if possible, even more impressed with this delicious woman. As the evening turned into night, Foxy held his head in her hands, averting her gaze so he wouldn't see the tears brimming in her big brown eyes. "Is it, and James believe me I wish it wasn't, but you know, almost time?"

Pausing to consider, James reluctantly replied, "Yes". He had no idea how to gauge when someone would be ready to travel back in time, for the first time. He remembered the professor's warning that it would make you feel like you were drunk. Well since he was drunk already, being twice as drunk seemed like as good a goal as any to move towards, to arrive in 1918 as. Foxy dolefully went to make some final preparations and James was left alone to mentally ready himself.

A minute later a topless Foxy crossed through to the bedroom on the far end of the room. This threw James' concentration for a loop and he realised, difficult as it may be, he needed to get away from all temptation as soon as possible. He wanted Foxy, badly, but the professor had warned 20/20 to warn D to warn him that, like a boxer or champion keg lifter, sex was absolutely forbidden close to the actual time traveling as James would need all his strength.

Contemplating the chain that message had taken and deciding there was a ninety percent chance that that wasn't what the professor had said at all, James stood up to follow Foxy into the bedroom.

"Undress, now." Wearing only silver sparkling stars over her nipples, Foxy seemed to have the same idea. Only after a second did James notice the Colt .45 trained on his liver. Petrified, he did as he was told. "And get into those." She waved the gun towards a pile of 1918-style clothes, fancy yet filthy just the way James wore them, with a holster sitting on top.

"There are some good vintage shops around here." Now it was her turn for fright. Quickly turning the handle of the Colt around, she offered it to his naked figure, "Oh, I'm so sorry, James. I didn't mean to scare you. Here, you might need this where you're going."

James dressed speedily, slinging the holster normally used for flasks around his shoulder. He took a step towards her outstretched hands and nearly fell over. As drunk as he was, James *knew* he was that drunk, and thus felt ready. They walked solemnly hand in hand to the bathroom. Foxy kissed him long and deep, James not wanting to let her go as he climbed into the tub. "Good luck, James."

"I'll be back soon, I promise, Foxy." He closed the door and punched in the numbers that would bring him back to the summer of 1918.

Almost instantaneously James found himself staring out the door of the telephone booth onto a dark patch of tall grass and bushes. He vaguely recalled multi-dimensional clocks spinning around his head and what seemed like a never-ending barrel jump. But he could not comprehend what had just happened or what was currently taking place. He somehow got the door open, and taking a tentative step out, spun around, around, and around again, finally falling flat on his face and blacking out on the hard dirt.

6 – Train of Drought

James Vagabond lifted his head slowly from the dust, barely able to hold it up for a second before crashing back into the ground with a thud. Coughing, he once again slipped into unconsciousness. This scene had been repeated five or six times since he had fallen from the telephone booth. Coming to again, he kept his head down until he was certain he could stand. This took quite a while, and without a drink it seemed even longer. It was dark again, or was it dark still? James had no idea how long he had been back in time. He never wore a watch, hating the sound of metal scraping glass when carrying an armful of bottles; this happened more than you would expect. Finally clambering to his feet, after the umpteenth failed attempt, he looked into the time machine but, rather puzzlingly, the device gave no indication of what time it was currently. Lengthening his gaze, he took in the miles of scrubland surrounding him. 'So this is 1918', he thought. At least it isn't black and white, as he had half-expected it to be.

James stood looking at the apparatus that had brought him to the past. He recalled Foxy's instructions to hide it safely for his return. 'How the hell am I going to do that?' He winced. Blood pounding behind his temples, eyes aching, and with his dry tongue clinging to the roof of his mouth, he had one of the worst hangovers he had ever experienced. With no one around to see him acknowledge this, James hung his head, clenching his eyes shut. He had to find a drink soon. When he once again opened his lids, he caught a glimpse of his reflection in the glass of the telephone booth, backed by the moonlight. Yes, falling in the dirt had greatly helped restore his former state of filth, before all those fancy showers aboard the Queen Bea damaged his image. This gave him the confidence he needed and he set to work immediately. The best way to conceal the time machine seemed to be to lower it down on its side and drag it into the bushes.

But the strain of tilting the booth to the ground caused him to perspire profusely. He half-expected to smell the Kiwi Quail Schnapps again, but to his surprise his sweat was quite alcohol-free. The professor had been right about evaporation and James shuddered at this terrible truth. Coaxing the machine about five feet, he collapsed to the ground, panting with great force. He squeezed his eyes closed again, trying to drain any remaining alcohol out of any possible duct. This action seemed to kickstart his brain.

"Bloody Mary!" Moving the machine might be disastrous when he returned to Ted Williams' house! Grunting and swearing, he pulled the booth back to the marks in the dirt showing its original location. His faulty thinking was evidence of the fact that he was sobering up. Noticing a grove of shady trees nearby, James set about gathering branches and leaves, camouflaging the callbox as best he could. Automatically scanning the ground for cigarettes, he remembered that he still had some butts in his pocket. Reaching in, first right then left, and not feeling the familiar hole inside, James recalled Foxy making him undress, the most disappointing time he had ever done so. In his new threads, without a single smoke or drink, James was at an all-time low. There was nothing for it but to find his way to a train station, get back up North and into the action.

Head throbbing and stomach churning, James' sole concern was finding a drink. After he had righted his body and mind, then he could worry about the other details of the operation. Bewildered by this wilderness, he began to curse himself for focusing only on Foxy as she drove him from the station. But there was no sense in pointless rebukes that would make him feel even worse. Decades doubtless would have changed the scenery and James couldn't imagine any man or woman who could concentrate on much else with Foxy around.

The night air was warm and hearing the distant purr of traffic, James headed in its direction. Visions of hijacking a beer delivery truck quickened his pace. Arriving at the road however, few cars, let alone trucks, were traversing it. He trudged on, not bothering to consider whether or not the vehicles that might come by would pick up a man dressed like himself, out in the middle of nowhere.

James Vagabond soon caught the faint clatter of creaking metal and what sounded acutely like feminine exclamations of pleasure. The noises seemed to be coming from a copse of palm trees twenty yards down an incline to his left, obscured from the main road. James crept stealthily towards the grove; if he was correct in his assumptions, there was more than a slight chance there would be alcohol there. Not to explore the situation would be folly. The elated womanly cries were growing louder and more forceful. Squinting, James could make out the shape of an antique car parked between the palms trees. Not antique here, he reminded himself, and reaching the trees now he saw that it was a convertible, conveniently with its top down. He craned his head, hoping to catch a glimpse of what was actually happening in the car.

Speaking wonders for James' predicament, voyeurism was the furthest thing from his mind. He was busy reasoning that even if she didn't have any alcohol in the vehicle, he might somehow be able to charm her into taking him closer to where a drink might be found, or even the train station. James risked being seen and stuck his head further out from behind the palm. It was an unnecessary precaution as he saw now both a man and woman, thoroughly wrapped up in what they were doing. As the man remained for the moment silent, James reckoned he had a little time yet. With her open mouth continuing its short bursts of delight and her jeweled hands running their fingers through her companion's hair and up and down his spine, James watched this woman's eyes. Satisfied they weren't likely to open, he formulated a plan. He didn't have to worry about the man, the chap was looking straight down into the leather of the front seat.

Without another thought, James snuck up to the side of the car, risking a quick peek around the interior. Sitting on the back seat was a re-corked bottle. It bore no label but James could sense it was red wine of a recent and perhaps local vintage, bearing the slightest hint of fruit but otherwise unknown to his palate. Mentally rubbing his hands together in delight, he now prepared for the tricky business of obtaining it. James reasoned that once inside the vehicle he would be fine and everything hinged on just one moment. Timing the man's thrusts, he began swaying along with them. When he was ninety-nine percent certain he had gotten the rhythm right, he vaulted up onto the edge of the auto with the next incoming heave.

"Oh Jay!" the girl exclaimed as Vagabond held himself upside-down in a handstand on the side of the car, before gently rolling down into the rear seat. In the next instant he slid onto the floor, grabbing the bottle and covering himself with a blanket. There are times in life one is truly thankful. And this, despite being years away from his own reality, in the terrifying unknown past of a foreign land, hiding on the floor beneath a copulating couple, was one of them. Pulling the cork out with the next moan, James passed an awkward few more minutes drinking under the blanket with the passenger seat repeatedly knocking into his legs.

When it was all over, James was even more grateful to have the wine in his hands, having no other choice than to listen to the tender whispers of spent lovers. Soon the girl straightened up, adjusting clothes and hat.

"That was wonderful Jay, but I really must be getting home."

The car promptly began to make its shaky way back to the main road. Feeling better now and slightly mischievous after a nearly full bottle of wine (it obviously hadn't taken very much to get this couple going), James laughed silently to himself over what he had just been through. Knowing it might soon be too late, he sat up quickly in the back seat, bellowing "Listen, old boy, would you mind terribly dropping me at the nearest train station?"

"AHHHHHHHHHHHH!" A different kind of scream now. The car, braking hard at this feminine ejaculation, skidded to a stop off the road again.

"Who the hell are you? Get out of my car this instant," the man known as Jay turned barking into Vagabond's face. But seeing such a sight herself, the girl began to blush a deep scarlet and, lowering her eyes demurely, offered James Vagabond a coy, welcoming smile. As Jay hopped out of the car, intent on physically removing James, the girl swiftly put her hand on his arm.

"No Jay, let's see what this man wants."

Jay stood shocked. "But Daisy..."

"Please, Jay." she batted her eyelashes at him.

"Oh alright," Jay spat, slamming the door as he climbed back in.

"Sorry to trouble you, folks," James Vagabond switched to his best American accent, "but I seem to have gotten a little lost and I just need to get to the railroad station." James smiled, slowly tucking the empty bottle out of view.

"A little lost?" Jay exclaimed, looking at the barren brush about them. "Wait a second, how long have you been back there anyway?" Jay's face grew red with embarrassment.

"Long enough," Vagabond replied coolly, thinking that there was no reason for this man to be ashamed; his performance had been perfectly adequate. With a deep sigh, Daisy began to fan her face with her right hand, overcome by James' response.

They rode on in an awkward silence until a train station came into view. Vagabond's mind quickly began to focus on his journey, "Listen, old boy -" he caught himself, though neither seemed to notice the British-ism spoken in James' now Americanised voice. "You wouldn't happen to have another bottle of wine on you? Or any alcohol at all?" he added, hopeful and trying not to sound too desperate.

"Sorry, old chap," Jay replied, "that was the last we had. Have to be careful nowadays, you know."

"Of course," James replied rather sullenly. Then his brain pricked up. These are *drinkers*! The first people he had come across after arriving back in time, drinking in the face of Prohibition. Maybe there was something in D's mixed-up plan of sending him so out of the way to Florida, that old 'secret drunken wisdom'. But then of course D could never have known, and James' vague agenda didn't include spending any more time in Florida than it took to get him out of it. But maybe, just maybe, he could sow some intoxicating seeds. "Listen," he started, "correct me if I'm wrong, but you two are against this whole Prohibition nonsense, right?"

"Oh it's just ghastly," Daisy seemed genuinely upset at its very mention. "Ghastly."

"Yes, a truly awful business," Jay emphasised as he turned into the station lot. James sensed he had to hurry.

"I agree. If only we could find a way to stop this thing. You wouldn't happen to know anyone in the Florida government, would you?"

Jay wrinkled his forehead as he shifted the car into park. "As a matter of fact my uncle is a good friend of one of the Senators, or something like that. Seems a decent enough fellow."

"Does your uncle drink?"

"Like a fish, old man, like a fish. It's him we pinched this wine from." Jay smiled.

"Talk to your uncle then. Tell him he needs to convince the Senator and the good people of Florida not to ratify the Amendment that will put Prohibition into place. It would be disastrous." Hopping out of the car in a much less grand way than he had entered, James shook Jay's hand. "And thanks for the ride." Daisy blew him a kiss as he turned to go, and James felt satisfied with himself. If only that was all it took to stop Prohibition. He had half a mind to head back to the time machine, go forward a few months and see if this short speech had done the trick. But then he caught himself, no assignment was ever that easy. And besides, he really needed another drink.

A quick reconnaissance of the station revealed it to be as dry as James' blistering throat. But Vagabond had found a train bound for Washington D.C., due to depart momentarily. Peering into the window of its restaurant carriage, it was much the same scene as the dusty environs outside. Wrestling with his conscience until the whistle blew, he concluded that this was nonetheless his best option, diving through the doors of a storage car moments before an inspector came to close them. James sighed as the train started down the tracks. In just the fifteen minutes since he had left Jay and Daisy, James Vagabond had felt the full horror of the time he had been sent back to. A sense of duty rushed through his blood and he was now more determined than ever to put an end to this madness.

He had chosen 1918, the year after Amendment 18 had been passed but when it was not yet ratified, because combating the passing of the amendment had seemed damned near impossible. It had gone through with a vote of 321-70. No, the best way to handle this situation, James Vagabond had thought, was to try and stop the ratification of the Amendment. Even this seemed a very long shot indeed. Forty-five of the forty-eight states had ratified it, with only Rhode Island having the good sense to vote against. Illinois and Indiana had not voted for it. The amendment needed 'several states'' legislatures to ratify and James was hoping that meant a high three-fourths, but most likely it was only two-thirds of the states. He knew he should've written it down. At least he was aware of what he was up against, James consoled himself, even if he didn't have a plan just yet.

It seemed unthinkably dark in the carriage, though a good deal of light shone through the windows. At this realisation of all he had left in front of him, Vagabond felt even the last drops of Jay's vino leaving his system. It was unthinkable that there would be no alcohol whatsoever on this train or, for that matter, in any given place on Earth. James began rummaging through the surrounding suitcases. A good three-quarters of an hour search proving fruitless, he found himself at a low enough ebb to settle for a two percent fruit-flavoured alcopop that hadn't even been invented yet, should one somehow now magically appear. This was truly a desperate situation. He wondered what other agents might do in his predicament but none of those men had ever faced what James was staring head on at now – the prospect of an hour or two without even access to a drink, and James shook with rage as he realised it might be a lot longer than that.

Feeling utterly defeated, James rifled through the luggage again to find the deck of cards he had glimpsed during his previous perusal. Not even the sight of vintage ladies' undergarments cheered him up. He took the pack and sat down in a parallelogram of moonlight on the floor. He began to shuffle, reflecting on how different this was from the Eurostar ride from Bruxelles to London. Then he had had alcohol, women, and baccarat. Now he was left alone with the cards in a cruel, foreign land. The bottom of the barrel. Except that there was no barrel. There wasn't even anyone else with whom to play Gin Rummy, his favourite card game. Sadly, he began to lay the cards out for a game of Solitaire. His play was slow, half-hearted, and he soon found himself wondering bitterly how you could turn Solitaire into a drinking game. A smile briefly broke his sombre expression as he realised you could take a drink for every card played, turned over, or even just looked at. The amusement faded quickly, though he mentally filed this version of the game away for a time when he could make use of it. A better time.

Suddenly there were no more cards left in his hand. James tried to read some sort of fortune in this but his heavy eyes flickered uncomprehendingly on the four neat stacks, leading up from Aces to Kings, and soon he fell asleep, head resting on his fist.

7 – Boots & Legs & Beers, Oh My!

Four days later James Vagabond stumbled off a train into the cool noontime breeze of Cleveland, Ohio. The trek had not been easy but at least he was now at his chosen destination. James had picked Cleveland as his first port of call the minute he read that the Women's Christian Temperance Union was formed here and that Ohio was also the birthplace of another great agency of evil – The Anti-Saloon League. As his feet hit the ground his nose was already picking up the scent of brewing hops and fermenting grapes. Following its lead, his walk now more of a restrained run, for the first time he was able to laugh at the mishaps of the preceding days.

James had awoken chin-deep in the cold sweat that had accumulated in his palm over the course of his slumber. The four Kings, one of each suit, seemed to be staring deep into his eyes, penetrating his soul. The King of Clubs even appeared to be winking at him. James had heard that this is what sometimes happens to people when they sober up. He shuddered and then blacked out again, coming to only when the train had stopped in Washington D.C.. He had no idea how long the train had been sitting there when he jumped out into the shadows, nor any clue how much time he spent roaming the rail yard. He could only remember the terrible shakes that wracked his body until he finally came across a man sitting with a bottle in another storage car on another train. The man was dressed very much like James himself and bearded to boot. James fervently hoped this wasn't a mirage. Patting and prodding the hobo to make sure he was real, James could've kissed this drifter when, all agiggle, the gent offered to share his grog. James drank ferociously.

"Hop on up, pardnah. Almost departin' time."

As if in a trance, James jumped up alongside this stranger, following him deeper into the compartment, both soon settling in for a long ride. The man - James never did catch his name - turned out to have quite a stash of alcohol on board. Getting up to every conceivable hijinx you can in a railway storage car – dancing, hide and seek, one-on-one football, synchronised mime, sometimes all at the same time - the party continued well on into the night and next day. Sometime the morning after that, as the two were enjoying the scenery from the opened doorway of the moving train, the hobo turned to James.

"Say, where you headin'?"

"Cleveland, I guess."

"Yee-haw! You gotta be kiddin'."

James raised his eyebrows in alarm, slowly shaking his head 'No'.

"See that out there, my friend? That's the fine state of Tay-haas, that is. And Cleveland…" The hobo grabbed a shotgun, firing at some passing birds. Pointing to one now squawking frantically at a right angle to the others, he continued, "Cleveland's up that ways. Yessirree." He calmly put down the gun. "I'm heading to Meh-hee-coh myself. Escaping before the whole country undrinks itself to death with this Prohibition baloney."

Alighting at the next stop to reverse his course – "Suit yourself, more booze for me," the soon-to-be expat replied to Vagabond's abundant apologies – James was nonetheless given a jug of tequila for his journey. Rather foolishly James drained its entire contents before even boarding the next train. Once again ransacking the suitcases, he could find neither cards nor secret canteen. And as if to add insult to injury, he was caught in a storm during a layover in North Carolina. So much for his artfully crafted appearance. Not that he would need it now, here, away from all he had ever known. It was only on the train from Baltimore to Cleveland that he had better luck. Rummaging through the luggage he came across two 25-cent pieces on the floor between two bags, which he pocketed quickly. Now jangling in his palm as he walked through 1918 Cleveland, James passed a shop window which read 'CIGARETTES 20¢'. London was very far away indeed - miles, decades. All of a sudden, a bolt of air raced up his nose, knocking his head back. The source of those sweet fumes! Looking up, a sign announced 'The Round Table' and James Vagabond walked through its door.

"This way! You're late again." A young man wearing an apron grabbed James' elbow, ushering him at a great speed through the door at the back of the room. James, appalled by this person's rude behavior, was about to say something to this effect when the young man explained, "Sorry, sir, it's just that you look like you are here to drink and we can't be too careful nowadays. Please tell me if I'm wrong."

Befuddled, not least by the mention of his not being on time, James sunk into the seat his young assailant now offered him. "No. That's correct."

The lingering look of confusion on James' face prompted the boy to continue. "We have to keep up the appearance of a restaurant out in front and so far no one has caught on to this secret room back here. Most folks use the entrance in the kitchen." He pointed to a doorway through which another young gentleman was carrying plates piled high with cabbage and meat. "But don't worry, to the casual observer it will simply appear that you were late for work washing dishes."

James looked around him. His spacious surroundings gave the impression of being inside the trunk of a giant oak tree. Plenty of round tables were spread about the floor, booths and benches clinging to the wooden walls, along with a few dartboards higher up, the latter unused for the moment. The people gathered here - and the room was almost at capacity - were all having a much better time than the crowd James had seen out front.

"I take it you're English then?" the young man half-asked, half-stated. Shaken by the commotion, James had spoken in his normal voice. He now considered that perhaps it was best this way, easily explaining his unfamiliarity with time and place.

"That is also correct."

"I'll fetch you a drink straight away then. Here's the deal, it's fifteen cents for a plate of grub but that includes a free glass of beer. The other way around used to be pretty common practice in America, but these are dark days indeed. The food's delicious though. We've got the best würst and sauerkraut this side of Hamburg."

James reached in his pocket, fingering the two quarters. "I've had rather a long trip. Bring me two."

"Two, sir?" The young man sounded as if he was having trouble understanding James.

"Yes, to start."

As the youth hurried away, James looked up at a rather grotesque noise emanating from one of the tables nearby. Following a stream of dark saliva through the air, James noticed the vast number of brass spittoons dotted about the floor. Instinctively and disappointingly feeling in his pocket for a cigarette butt, James found comfort in the sight of an overflowing ashtray lurking in the shadows to his side. Choosing a good-sized end, unfiltered as they all seemed to be, and lighting it from the candle on the table, he glanced about to see if anyone was watching. He needn't have worried, but as this was the first large social setting he'd encountered since traveling back in time, he was feeling slightly self-conscious. His backbone was greatly bolstered upon catching the brilliant glare off the mugs of beer coming his way. The first was in James' hand before it reached the table. Starting back towards the kitchen again, the young man assured him, "I'll be right back with your food."

"You better make it two more," James belched.

The youngster turned and stared in amazement at the empty glasses now upside-down on the tabletop, incongruous slices of foam-covered limes encircled by their rims. He swallowed. "Would you like two more lunches also?"

"Why not?" James smiled. The young man hurried away and soon brought two more glasses of beer, pale green citrus wedges floating in the froth, and then four lunch plates. As the waiter placed the dishes on the table, James once again felt the fifty cents in his pocket. Rough calculations in his head – four meals at fifteen cents apiece – forged a charming smile to beam from his features. "You better run a tab."

Shoveling sizeable forkfuls into his mouth, James' drinking pace slowed to only regional championship speed. He peered around the room at all the men and women eating and drinking, enjoying themselves as was only right. He wondered who they were, what they were doing to stop Prohibition. James was unclear as to the exact history of the U.S. Drinking Service but knew there were at least a dozen smaller agencies scattered about the country by the time 'the noble experiment' began. It was most likely this trial of error that had spurred them on to work harder, becoming what they were today, well, his today. But without any means of finding them or making contact if he did, he could not count them into his plans. James drank deep, hoping that if he succeeded in his mission, it wouldn't damage the growth of the American Service too greatly. After all, DRINKS and SUDS were allies of sorts, working together on assignment when necessary. He hoped too, and not for the first time, that he understood the way the United States government functioned. He had applauded President Wilson for vetoing the National Prohibition Act, and the fact that Congress overrode the veto embittered Vagabond enormously, even now, before it had actually happened. The waiter was passing by again and James called out, "Another drink, please! But that's enough food for now."

"Two?"

"Why not?"

James Vagabond had been sitting in the back room for over an hour. He was truly enjoying himself, finishing up his tenth beer. Sitting amongst the stacks of plates, empty mugs, and inexplicable pieces of citrus, James was somewhat startled to notice the kitchen door open, his waiter whispering to a tall well-dressed man with lustrous black hair and matching beard. They were both looking in James' direction. 'Oh no', James thought, 'time to pay up'. More mental arithmetic told him he was already a dollar short but he had no intention of curtailing his drinking activities any time soon. The well-dressed man, whom James considered must be the proprietor of the place, walked over coolly, stopping just the other side of James' table. Vagabond waited.

The big man loomed over him. "Well, well, well. A Limey in King Arthur's court." His hand shot out. "Welcome to America. Lance says you've had a long trip. I'll bet. The name's Miller, Arthur Miller, but everyone around here calls me King Arthur. I own this place, you see, as well as most of the other finer drinking establishments about town."

James Vagabond stood up, warmly shaking Arthur Miller's hand. "James," he introduced himself.

Arthur looked at James standing perfectly straight, then down at the ten empty glasses on the table. "FFFUHhuhuhuhahaha!" Roaring a hearty laugh that ripped from his lips down the great man's throat to finally shake his protruding belly, he then bellowed, "Lance, get this man a gin! After all, aren't you British required to drink it by law?"

Arthur's good nature beamed, his mirth still rumbling through his stomach. James relaxed, thinking about what Arthur had just said. Yes, of course, what a good idea for a piece of legislation. He'd have to remember to tell D about it when he got back. King Arthur continued as the gin arrived, "Of course I make this stuff myself. Nowadays they've started to call it 'Bathtub Gin.'" James visibly shuddered. He had had quite enough baths on this adventure already. Arthur caught James' concern. "Don't worry, James, I have a more sophisticated method of distillation. And I'll be damned if you can distinguish it from your British variety."

Downing the shot, James smiled, "Exquisite." He could of course discern the difference – North American juniper berries for a start - but he would never let on to this hospitable man. And indeed the drink had been delicious.

"What did you think of the food?" King Arthur patted him on the back.

"Excellent, excellent. Lance was certainly correct, best würst and sauerkraut this side of Hamburg." James, for the first time since finishing his fourth heaping plate, thought of the sheer magnitude of what he had just eaten. Perhaps that's why I only feel a slight buzz, he reasoned.

"You know, a lot of this Prohibition talk is being bolstered by the anti-German sentiment running through this country right now," Arthur's face grew grave. "Most ridiculous thing I've ever heard. As if the Germans are the only ones who make beer! Thank heavens the war's ending though. All the grain being rationed to make bread for the soldiers instead of whiskey for the dying. No doubt you have something like that in your country. But just think that all the men who fought for our great nation will be coming home, from places like France no less, to find their own country going dry. It saddens the soul." Arthur wiped a tear from his eye. "Lance bring another beer for our friend. Or would you prefer the gin? Or both?" He was soon smiling again. James smiled too. "Both it is," shouted Arthur. "You'll have to forgive me for not joining you but ever since the troubles started I never drink during business hours. Folks out there," he gestured towards the front room, "think I'm a respectable business man, at least by their definition. But say, what are you doing tonight?"

Considering his mission for a second, James replied honestly, "I have no plans."

"Jolly good, as I believe you say. If you'd care to join me, I'll show you around. Take you to one of my after-hours emporiums.

They're calling them speakeasies now, since the saloons have been shut down. That damn League! It's better this way though. Saloons were men only, but there's plenty of women coming to the speakeasies these days." Arthur's rosy cheeks shone with salacious delight. "Meet me here tonight. Say around ten. That's what time the front closes."

James smiled, "If you don't mind, I think I'll just sit right here until then. It's been quite a journey. And as long as I can keep drinking..."

"Of course, of course," Arthur grinned. "Good man. And don't worry about a thing, it's all on the house."

James' sigh of relief continued long after Arthur had disappeared through the kitchen door.

When King Arthur returned at ten o'clock he was carrying a glass of pale amber liquid with him, which he handed to James. "Try this." James raised it in a toast to his benefactor. Before he could swallow, the mouthful of fluid was propelled straight into the nearest spittoon.

"What in blazes?" James shrieked.

"FFFUHhuhuhuhah!" Arthur doubled over laughing, clutching his sides and panting for breath. Patting James on the shoulder, he repeated apologetically, "I'm sorry, my friend, truly sorry. Please forgive me. That," nodding to the spittoon instead of the glass, "is what we call Wort, or near-beer. It's legal to serve and we have it up front because it is less than 0.5 percent alcohol. But you just add yeast, wait a little while, and you're all set. This is what society is coming to. Wort, sacramental wine, medicinal alcohol, the only things left that are legal. A shame. A crying shame." He bowed his head for a minute, sombre, before bouncing back to his jovial self. "C'mon. Let's get going."

The two men walked out into the cool night air, wending their way down the shadowy street. James was feeling quite himself again and glad to have found such an understanding companion. Especially one who also seemed to run this city's liquor business. "Cigarette?" Arthur offered. James was now even more endeared to him. Twisting and turning, they shortly came to a non-descript door. A panel slid open at eye level and King Arthur smiled. "On any given evening, a password is required but this is my club and you are my guest." Arthur continued over the sounds of bolts being thrown and locks turning. "We haven't given this place a name yet, seems to work best that way, but everyone calls it Camelot. Up the street I also have a nice little joint, The Red Garter, used to be The Red Garter Saloon before the saloons went out. I'll take you there another night. With the way you've been drinking today it might be a waste of a bed."

Arthur slapped James on the back, roaring his usual laugh. Normally James would have been deeply insulted by this affront to both his manhood *and* his drinking ability, but there was something in the way Arthur put it that made James laugh too. And who was he to argue with a man who let him drink all day for free and was now taking him to drink some more? The door opened and they hurried inside, the multiple locks turning into place immediately behind them.

As it drifted amongst the soft lights, sultry jazz, and sounds of genuine debauchery, the lingering greyish-blue smoke caressed James lightly by way of greeting as he stepped into Camelot. Arthur waved warmly to patrons in every corner, clearing the way towards the best seat in the house. Before they could even take their chairs, two large libations appeared in front of them. "We call these Excaliburs. Sometimes I don't even know what's in them." James wondered what Arthur could possibly have meant by this curious remark, watching the big man down his entire glass in one go, immediately ordering another one. Making up for all those dry hours imposed on him at work. "This is rather a slow night tonight," Arthur explained, "Hope you're not too disappointed."

"Of course not," James replied in between sips, "just what I need." He could see what Arthur meant about the drink. A veritable rainbow of flavours and proofs, each taste differing slightly from the one before.

Settling in, Arthur began to explain to James about the growing bootlegging industry. "The trouble is they can't enforce these laws and I don't truly believe anyone really wants to stop drinking anyway. A lot of people are feeling betrayed about the way the phrase 'intoxicating liquors' is being defined. I mean sure, to play devil's advocate, if I was drunk enough I might be able to see a case for banning whiskey, gin, vodka, you know, the hard stuff." James sat up, all his senses coming alive. He had been trained to search out the exits at such talk. "Sorry, James, I'm not serious of course, just trying to get into these madmen's heads. But everyone feels cheated now that beer and wine are included. That just doesn't make any sense. And you know what? Now hard liquor consumption is only going to increase. You see, you have to move beer in large quantities, which can be very dangerous, easy to get hijacked, killed, or caught by the police. But hard liquor, since it's more potent, can be transported in much smaller amounts and stored in just about anything."

Arthur made a wide sweeping motion with his right hand, taking in the entire room. "Around this bar tonight we have collected some of the finest bootleggers, moonshiners, and rumrunners this country has ever produced. See that gentleman over there with the glasses and cane?" James' jaw dropped as Arthur pointed to the spitting image of 20/20. How had he managed to…? Had D's favourite agent been there the whole time in the phone booth with James? James had been drunk but surely not too intoxicated to notice another man traveling alongside him in congested quarters back through the temporal ether. And 20/20 had once or twice before left James face down in the dirt for the sake of a successful operation. On his guard and clutching his Excalibur with all his might, James guzzled it down nervously.

"Well that's Moonbeam Jim. And that cane is hollow as the day is long, filled to the brim with medicinal whiskey he procured from a doctor this very afternoon. His motto is 'Speak easy and carry a big stick!' FFFUHhuhuhuhahaha!" Arthur slapped the table repeatedly, bellowing out his loveable laugh. As if in answer,

Moonbeam Jim, his hearing finely tuned, raised his dark glasses and winked in their direction. For the first time in years James nearly choked on a drink, such was his relief that Moonbeam's uncovered features bore little if any resemblance to his friend back in London.

Another round of Excaliburs arrived as Arthur's roar subsided. "Yep, you can hide alcohol in just about anything – chiseled-out books, the heels of your shoes, we've been installing secret second gas tanks on cars, false-bottomed suitcases of course..."

"How about a false-bottomed baby pram? Or putting it in a teapot? That way you could serve it at your restaurant," James interrupted.

"Fella," Arthur stared at James with great admiration, "you just earned yourself all the free alcohol you want. Maybe I'll take you to that cathouse tonight after all." Arthur quickly finished his Excalibur, signaling for more. "Mankind's imagination never fails to impress me. Up in Michigan they even have an underwater cable system to carry booze across the river bottom from Canada. The sunken houseboats hide it perfectly. Mind you, we used to supply Michigan with her drink before they passed the law here as well."

"Genius, utter genius," James nodded his approval.

"We got some real geniuses in this state too." Arthur pointed to a dark corner. "See that feller over there, sitting by himself, all quiet-like, minding his own business? Well, that's Mr. Daniel Jackson. Was one of the first of us, delivering whiskey in a milk truck. Now has a line of taxicabs with false-bottomed floors and bottles even taped inside the spare wheels. Hell of a man. And over there," Arthur motioned to a more lively table on the opposite side of the room, "those two men with the ladies on their laps? Why the one on the left's none other than Mark "Match" Maker, and on his right's his cousin, Mark "Boiler" Maker. They're up to all sorts of tricks."

The evening carried on in much the same style. Countless Excaliburs were consumed and James was thoroughly exhausted when closing time rolled around. It had been his first full day of drinking at his destination and whatever was in the Excaliburs rendered them extremely potent. James sensed his mission now in progress and looked forward to the coming days. It would be a refreshment course; getting him back into shape as he'd been meaning to do this whole trip, as no doubt he would need to be in order to accomplish his objective. The two men walked out together, Arthur's bear-like arm hugging James' shoulders to him in good cheer. Back at The Round Table, King Arthur took his leave.

"I trust I'll be seeing you tomorrow, Sir James?"

"You have my word, m'lord." As the King turned the corner, James Vagabond stumbled into the alleyway conveniently situated behind The Round Table, falling into a deep, contented sleep.

8 – Death of a Salesman

The next week passed in much the same manner as James Vagabond's first day in Cleveland. Waking up in the alley around noon, he would knock at The Round Table's secret kitchen entrance and settle down to lunch and a day of drinking. He saw no reason to visit any other establishment. At night, after Arthur Miller finished working, the King would take James to one of his various after-hours clubs, usually ending up at Camelot. James knew that he had been to The Red Garter at least twice, as he had awoken there on two consecutive mornings, confused and alone in a comfortable bed. There had been positions a-plenty he had not known the name of, although he did faintly recall that when the beekeeping uniform changed hands for the third time, someone in the room had suggested that that particular act be known as 'The Beekeeper'. The rest was foggy bliss. His only real impression of the place itself was of taking his leave through a hallway littered with lace and reception area blushed deepest crimson. King Arthur had also brought him, when their assorted drinking companions were passing out in the early hours, to the various basements and warehouses containing Arthur's vast distilleries and the vehicles that transported their end results all over creation. The King had a very far-reaching and profitable operation in place. Superbly run too, it seemed to James.

On the following Friday, Arthur approached James at their usual ten o'clock meeting spot, speaking seriously at first. "Friend, I'm taking you someplace new this evening. We've been spending too much time at Camelot, it's high-time you experienced The Shining Armory." Quickly the gravity faded from King Arthur's face. "FFFUHhuhuhuha! Come on, Sir James, you'll love it."

Walking to this new nightspot, King Arthur explained the legend behind its name. "No one remembers what it was called before

I bought it, or if it even existed as a watering hole back then, but it's always been known as 'The Shining Armory'. One night, ages ago, our beloved barmistress Gwen concocted this deliciously potent melange. Again, don't ask me what was in it; I only drink them. Well, you light this elixir on fire before throwing it back and since all the walls are mirrored… You get the picture. No one remembers what we referred to them as while we drank them but, oh my, that next morning. About ten of us, yours truly included, woke up face down on the bar, and near Moonbeam's head was a cocktail napkin with some illegible scrawl written on it. The only words we could make out were 'armored car bomb' Oh how we laughed. As good a name as any for this dangerous drink, we decided. Boy oh boy, did I have a hangover that day, and had to be at work an hour later. Ah, here we are. Time for you to meet its maker."

Arriving at an unmarked door, they went through the same clandestine routine with the sliding panel and numerous bolts and locks, a procedure James could still not fathom. All this to get a drink! Except for the mirrors on the walls and the beautiful woman in white behind the bar, James could see little difference between the interior of Camelot, or any of the other places King Arthur had brought him to this past week, and The Shining Armory. "Gwen, my dear, meet the good Sir James. He hails from Great Britain."

James brought her offered hand to his lips, placing a kiss above her multitudinous rings. "Enchanted." And he meant it. The alabaster curve of her cheek, the waves of fine golden hair, the fact that she had five bottles laced between her fingers ready to pour. But peering into those sky blue eyes, it was obvious, and rare indeed, that there was no spark between her and Vagabond. James felt relief, sensing in this woman more than just allegiance to the king of these clubs. But the strength emanating just from those fingertips and limitless reserves of cool in her gaze told James that if she was anyone's, she was her own.

The Armored Car Bombs began to roll, James' bearing the distinct flavour of lime. It had been quite a while since James had last downed a blazing beverage, being of the mind that it burns up the alcohol and is therefore a tragic waste. But he was also never one to turn down a free drink and he quickly dismissed any qualms from his thoughts. With their tiny lights flickering from the mirrors, these petite blasts of inspiration soon had James Vagabond raising a silent toast to his old driver. Lighting a new smoke from the flame dancing atop his glass, he then threw back the shot, Ernst-style, cigarette hanging from lips. Another gulp involuntarily followed, revealing his surprise at his own grace. He had half-expected a soggy smoke to drop into his lap, setting himself on fire and spilling his drink in the process. James quickly ordered another Armored Car Bomb, then several more as the women of the bar lined up to have their Petite Cannons and Turkish Trophies lit. But soon King Arthur pushed his way through the gathered crowd of buxom beauties, all drinking in earnest, and pulled James over to a table in the corner.

"James, no doubt you've noticed my mood is a little dark tonight, though I daresay these Armored Car Bombs are helping a great deal" Arthur, himself now drinking with a Player's Navy Cut betwixt his lips, looked at Vagabond gravely. James nodded, acknowledging that the situation must be serious. "There's a party tomorrow night. Though how they dare to call it that beggars belief. These people already have the word 'league' under siege. Its connotations of oceans of booze are going out with the tide. And 'temperance' does not mean 'abstinence'."

Arthur shuddered, and James felt the room shake. "I've told you before that the non-drinkers of this state think that I'm on their side. They have no idea what I get up to, and if all goes well I'll be able to bring about their destruction from within. But I've yet to figure out what form this will take and I'm still forced to attend these sorry soirces. Tomorrow night's an important one, lots of bigwigs from the W.C. Temperance Union and that evil of all evils, the Anti-Saloon..." Arthur spat. "...League. I hate to do this to anybody, and under normal circumstances I would never ask, but you seem very intuitive when it comes to drinking. It's in your blood, and maybe you can see something that I don't. Some way in to end this insanity of 'a clean and sober nation'. I hate to ask, and like I say it will be more tedious than a teetotal Tantalus...but would you consider coming along with me? A reconnaissance mission of sorts." An almost pleading look crossed Arthur Miller's brow.

James stared his friend dead in the eye and smiled. He knew he had been right to follow his nose to the scent of this man and his alcohol. He gripped Arthur's shoulder purposefully. "Of course I will, Arthur. Of course. Don't worry. After all you've done for me this week, I owe you at least this. And I too would like to see this madness banished from the world."

King Arthur let go a mighty sigh of relief, followed by one of his signature laughs. He clasped James' hand on his shoulder. "Thank you, my friend. Now let's get back to business." He waved to the waitress for another round of Armored Car Bombs.

Morning found them in the manner Arthur had described from the glorious history of this particular beverage, face down on the scorched bar, along with twenty or so other carousing casualties. James awoke ten minutes before anyone else, lifting his head and wiping his own pile of drool off thc countertop before helping himself to a breakfast beer. Upon opening his eyes, Arthur followed suit, but there was a sadness in his voice when he spoke.

"I'm not sure if I mentioned this last night but we're going to have to stay sober for the rest of today. We can't let anyone at the party suspect anything this evening." James bit his tongue. He had completely forgotten that he had agreed to attend any function, let alone a dry one. Arthur quickly added, after seeing the look on James' face. "Don't worry, as soon as we get outta there tonight, James, we'll come back here and drink 'til Monday morning. And you can keep going long after that! C'mon, let's have one more before we're off."

After finishing their beers, Arthur led James to The Red Garter. Pointing to a door on the ground floor, he mumbled, "Let's get some real sleep," his large frame continuing on upstairs. James stumbled into the room he was told to, falling onto a bed he felt certain he had slept in before. He awoke hours later to the clang of creaking mattresses, girlish giggles, and Arthur's booming laugh. "FFFUHhuhuhuhah!" James' shoes and socks had been removed, his shirt hung loose, and his trousers were slung over the back of a red velvet chair in the corner. He couldn't recall if this was his own doing.

A heavily scented brunette in a blood-coloured corset sat pulling on black stockings in front of the dressing table. She didn't offer any answers, simply smiling as she relayed the message, "King Arthur awaits your presence." James rubbed his eyes, continuing to do so as he left the room.

"Well, well, well," Arthur, refreshed in purple silk dressing gown, a gold crown atop his raven locks, bellowed as James strolled into the lobby. "Had a good rest, Sir James?" He laughed warmly, patting James on the shoulder. "James, I hate to keep being the bearer of bad news but I've noticed you've got some kind of sentimental attachment to these clothes you keep wearing. But they're not going to pass muster tonight. And neither is that beard."

Vagabond visibly cringed.

"Okay, okay, calm down, James. You can keep the beard, but we're going to have to trim it for you. Girls!" Arthur called. Two tall, slim beauties appeared from behind a curtained doorway. The dirty blonde on the left's hair was piled high on her head, two intriguing curls falling either side of her emerald eyes. She wore chocolate knee-high leather boots and cream-coloured lace undergarments that you could barely tell were there. The brown bob of the woman on the right curved in under her chin, her face a freckled teardrop. A peach slip hung from her shoulders, so small it fully revealed matching suspender belt and stockings.

"Don't worry, Sir James. We have the necessary attire waiting for you in the back. These lovely ladies will clean you up and help you to relax a little before we leave. This is Cinnamon," he motioned to the blonde, who curtseyed. "And this is Sinammon with an 'S'."

Sinammon fixed James with her deep brown eyes and let forth a long, slow hiss.

"Girls, take him back and get him ready. Sugar and Spice will be there to help out as well." The ladies wrapped their arms over James', leading him through the crimson curtains. Just before Vagabond was fully enveloped, King Arthur called out again, "Oh, and James, don't think I haven't seen that gun you've been hiding under your arm. You had better leave it here. We don't want any trouble tonight. I'll give it back to you later."

Arthur held out his hand. Reaching under his jacket, James had almost forgotten Foxy's Colt .45 in the holster normally reserved for carrying his flask. For a moment he bitterly regretted having to leave that flask in Florida, back in the future. Alcohol-evaporating time travel, Prohibition parties, whatever would they think of next? James shrugged his shoulders, trustingly placing the gun in Arthur's hand, and turned once again to follow his clean-up crew.

At six o'clock, dressed to the nines, James Vagabond emerged from the deep red drapes. He was tired but calm, ready to face the difficult task ahead. All four ladies had made bathing as acceptable an experience as it was ever going to get, trimmed all the character out of his beard, and meticulously cleaned his teeth and tongue after he opted for one last secret shot of gin. Arthur Miller, dressed much the same as Vagabond in a stylish, but not overly so, black tuxedo, met James at the door. The two men nodded to each other before proceeding outside to the waiting taxicab. They rode on in eerie silence, each contemplating what they were about to confront this evening. In an effort to lighten the mood, King Arthur spoke, "You know, it's a real shame, James. The whole bottom of this car could get everyone at Camelot nicely drunk three times over tonight. Right under these floorboards, a fully stocked bar. But we must think of the long run."

James smiled. He wanted to reassure Arthur that it would turn out right, that they'd defeat this thing. Then he sat back, looking out the window, his conflicting emotions raging about his being. The thought of so much alcohol positioned so close with the prospect of not being able to drink any for at least a couple of hours perturbed him greatly. All too bitterly did he recall the trials of his train journeys. On the other hand, this cab they rode in, seemingly a fairly common appurtenance amongst the bootleggers, far outdid the paltry refrigerators of his London service. Impressed, and with the knowledge that these bottles would be waiting right here for him, James knew he must consider the bigger picture.

The vehicle, which bore no indication of being a taxi tonight, pulled up a long dark drive, parking beside other cars with waiting chauffeurs. "See you later, Mitch." Arthur patted the driver's shoulder as they took their leave. Stepping out into the cool night air, James Vagabond surveyed his surroundings. A large grey house presented itself on top of a small hill. Sombre light shone through its lower windows and James could see the slowly moving silhouettes of a good-sized crowd inside. The top floor was a murky black, as if all vigour had faded from the healthiest stout. Encircling three-quarters of the yard, an unnaturally still wood descended back on all sides. Silence hung over the scene as if daring one to pop a cork or even let loose an audible sip. Arthur and James turned towards one another, reluctant acceptance of what they must do flickering in each of their eyes. Never before in James' life had he felt the urge to hold another man's hand, but he desperately wanted to now. Fear gripped him in full force. Vagabond swallowed silently, steadying his nerve, and the two men proceeded with caution to the front door.

A woman's expressionless face greeted them after just one ring of the doorbell resonated out into the night. "Ah, Mr. Miller," she shifted a frigid hand, the pale digits protruding only slightly from the sleeve of the severe black frock covering her skeletal frame. Arthur took her fingers in his, bowing before them but only gesturing a kiss. "And who is this?" she demanded to know, visibly alarmed.

"Do not worry, Mrs. Sourpuss. And please call me Arthur, like my friends do. Allow me to introduce James. He is visiting me from London. An old friend of the family." He turned towards Vagabond. "James, this is Mrs. Amaretto Sourpuss, our gracious hostess." James in turn bowed low and took the hesitantly offered hand, letting his lips grace it lightly.

Mrs. Sourpuss blushed, the colour quite noticeable on her ghostly cheeks. "Oh please. Since we're all friends…" she paused, thinking through the consequences of what she was about to propose, "…call me Amy." And after further consideration added, "I'll have to tell my husband to as well." She laughed, James thought, though unsure exactly what the sound she emitted was, and guided them into the main room.

They passed an elegant stairway that led up the left-hand side of the foyer, crossing over to various shadowy doors on the right of the floor above. A red velvet rope was positioned across the bottom of the steps. James marveled that this might be all it took to keep partygoers from gaining access to the bedrooms. Turning left before the stairs and proceeding through the large open doorway into the ballroom, Mrs. Sourpuss announced, "Well, here we are. Please help yourself to a drink. I have some business to attend to." Amy marched off, oblivious to James' bulging eyes at her use of the word 'drink'. But Arthur quickly filled him in regarding the purplish-red liquid in the punch bowl at the far end of the room.

"Now don't get excited James. That stuff just sittin' so pretty on that table over there, like it wasn't deceiving anybody, is what we call 'Vine-Glo'. It's just grape juice. I don't think these people have realised yet that after sixty days it ferments and turns into the real deal. I've been trying to figure out how we can use that to our advantage in the long game. But now let's split up and see if we can make some progress."

As Arthur strolled over to a group of solemn-looking businessmen, James stood for a moment by the doorway taking in the scene. The ballroom was gigantic, plenty of open space separating the not inconsiderable crowd, who had splintered off into threes and fours. To James' immediate right was a life-size bronze statue of a stern-looking someone named Brother Kenneth Tapp. Further down that side of the room was an ornate fireplace surrounded by sofas and a divan the colour of curdled milk, and in the far corner stood a podium bearing a three-foot hatchet sculpted from broken glass. The paintings that hung about the walls caused James much emotional distress – saloons on fire, devastated barley fields, bottles sitting in prison cells - all seeming to suck the light from the room. He moved off to investigate the Vine-Glo.

Arms shaking in unconscious protest, James ladled the fallacious liquid from its crystal bowl into a small – pointless, he considered – cup. Disappointing sip followed disappointing sip eventually flowing into a fantasy of being back in the time machine to transport himself sixty days into the future. James stood behind the banquet table for quite some time, lost in reverie, mindlessly sampling each of the desserts on the off-chance that one might turn out to be rum cake. He had no such luck. Mrs. Amaretto Sourpuss walked by occasionally, shooting him a quick smile, painful lines creasing her eyes and forehead as her lips strained against the tension exerted by the tight bun she wore in her hair. James began to notice covert glances from other ladies dispersed about the party, their lips lingering over their glasses of Vine-Glo. James smiled back, winking at a rate that might be considered blinking, and watched their faces flush like a pomegranate martini. But would seducing these women - and it wouldn't be fair not to include all of them - really help his cause? 'So why don't you ladies call off this whole Prohibition balderdash and we'll go upstairs?' he mentally rehearsed. The crystals of a chandelier, one of three hung about the room, chimed softly overhead as if the bedrooms were welcoming this plan of action; long, long absent from within their walls. James looked up, suppressing a shudder. Something wasn't right about this place. It was downright spooky that despite the high ceilings and incredible size of the room, such a heavy quiet persisted inside. And without intimate knowledge of what could be lurking in its dark dry depths, James considered that perhaps tonight was not the time to attempt to shag it back to health.

Aware now that for some minutes he had been standing quite as still as the statue facing him across the room, James moved to the end of the banquet table, closer to the front windows, so as not to arouse any suspicion that he might've sobered himself up into a coma. Would anyone think that? It occurred to James that this wagon he was on was heading straight for Paranoia, Indiana. He shook his head to call himself back to reality, continuing this gesture, slowed down and with mouth open, as a shocked reaction to the conversation he now found himself overhearing.

Four sombre men, a good combined 180 years older than James, each in dull black evening dress with thin white beards trickling down from what was left on their pates, stood cataloguing the number and types of sins, if these could even been called such a thing, each had committed in the past week and the astoundingly ferocious punishments the men inflicted upon themselves by way of retributions not even disguised as penance. Marek Jetski, noticing and approving of the additional condemnation provided by James' noggin, called Vagabond over and introduced his colleagues Upton Featherbottom, Walter Marketcrash, and Gustav Witheredspoon, before continuing, "…now the police officer hadn't seen me jaywalking so I had to cross back again, being sure not to act so abysmally this time but still I was powerless to impatience, a transgression I'll come to later, Featherbottom," he added as that man reared himself up to pounce, "and inform the law how dreadfully I had just behaved. Had to give that honourable protector of our community – and it took much cajoling – fifty dollars to let me spend the night in a jail cell. By no means filthy enough either…"

His three cohorts nodded with a strange mixture of approval and disgust. James followed suit, adding in 200 proof puzzlement to his expression.

Mr. Featherbottom cleared his throat, which seemed to raise a bushy eyebrow high on his forehead. "And what did you do about the bribery then, Jetski?"

"Locked myself in the shed the following night when they insisted I leave the prison. Slept on the cold ground. Came down with the most troublesome bronchial affliction after that. Was spitting up – "

Walter Marketcrash chimed in, "Twenty lashes for that, I would hope."

Mr. Witheredspoon looked at Marketcrash as if he'd lost all moral backbone. "At least, I would imagine. I wouldn't have left the shed, myself. And thirty lashes whilst on the cold, hard ground, shocking me out of any sleep that might come."

Marketcrash trying to make up credibility in his companions' eyes. "Quite, Mr. Witheredspoon. That's what I did when I first *heard* about jaywalking."

James sensed that it was his turn to say something. The need not to appear weak was palpable between these four men. Just when he thought this world couldn't get any more foreign, James was now required to fabricate believable misdemeanors and rectifications, as his real offences, even those of the past 10 hours, would surely shock these gents into heinous tortures self-inflicted upon their persons for the crime of simply hearing such delight in debauchery. Complicating matters, the only words that came to mind, as he felt all eyes turn towards him, were 'I once saw three girls giving each other *forty* lashes. We were on the train from Brussels to London...' But just at that moment Mrs. Amaretto Sourpuss walked over, lightly placing a freezing hand on his forearm.

"James. You simply must tell me all about London. Is it as dry as it is here?" She began to lead him away from this cluster of contrition. "Come, let's have a drink." James swallowed the bubble of sadness that burst in his throat at such a ridiculous offer. Mrs. Sourpuss sliding her right forefinger coyly along the edge of the banquet table as James made his way back behind the punch bowl. He caught Mr. Featherbottom's eyes scrutinising him intensely before moving back to whatever Marketcrash was arsekissingly confessing.

"Enjoying the party, James?" Amaretto Sourpuss asked, her voice attempting casual calm and failing miserably.

"Yes, Mrs. Sourpuss."

"Call me Amy like we decided," she shot back, harsher than she wished to convey. Moving closer to where James was reluctantly pouring himself a cup of Vine-Glo, "How are you finding our country in its time of great change? It is truly wondrous what we've accomplished, purging the agents of sin from our shores. Don't you think?" Her eyelashes fluttered like wounded birds.

James looked down into his soft drink. "Ummmmm, yyyyyyyyes," came the elongated reply that Amy Sourpuss took to be slow English seduction. For the first time in his entire life James Vagabond had told a lie regarding his love of alcohol. A great sense of remorse came over him. Even as a child, playing under a table in the pub, he had felt duty-bound to tell the truth of what was in his glass, and if it be milk he would say it was milk. Mrs. Sourpuss moved closer.

"It's so nice to meet a man who doesn't drink," she smiled.

Just then the doorbell rang, obscuring any noise of James grinding his teeth. Mrs. Sourpuss, obviously frustrated, exclaimed, "Darnit! Will you please excuse me, James?"

Vagabond let out a vast sigh of relief. A pleasurable sense of freedom coursed through his limbs but he opted to stay just now behind the table, obscuring any signs of a perverse excitement Mrs. Sourpuss had also managed to arouse in him.

After some minutes that James spent focusing on detumescence, Arthur strolled up next to him at the punch bowl. "Any progress, Sir James?"

"I'm sorry, Arthur, I just can't seem to think clearly here. You?"

"No, I'm afraid this evening has been somewhat of a waste. But I promise you that won't diminish the way we're going to make up for it." Arthur laughed a quieter version of his signature laugh. "Just a few more minutes and then we can leave, get back to real life."

As if on cue, the lights in the house extinguished, plunging them into darkness. James immediately dove in front of the punch bowl, out of an instinct to protect any possible alcohol in the surrounding area, making sure the arc of his fall covered as much of the table as he could. That is, after all, where the bottles would be if this were a normal party of rational human beings, with extra provisions stashed underneath. A shot rang out and James stiffened as he heard Arthur scream and a curious thud hit the floor. He cursed not having his Colt .45 on him but James knew it would only make matters worse if he were seen to be carrying a gun now. Rapid footsteps resounded in the distance, the front door slammed shut, and a car screeched out of the long circular drive. A confused murmur arose amongst the guests as the lights came back on.

James crawled over to where Arthur had collapsed on the ground, the great man clutching his chest, shaking and gasping for breath. Blood was darkening the King's bland dress shirt. Tears clouded James' eyes as he lifted the dying man's head onto his lap, intoning with a warmth he had not felt for some time, "I'm so sorry, my friend".

With his last breath and blood dripping from his lips, King Arthur Miller managed one last hearty bellow and spat "What the fffff...." But the final syllable never materialised.

9 – Cherry Waters

James Vagabond sat nursing an Excalibur in the back room of The Round Table, mentally going over the events of the previous evening for the hundredth time. 'Who could possibly have done this?' he asked himself, staring forlornly into the cave of yet another empty glass, suds slipping sadly down its sides. The initial police enquiries brought nothing except a parade of patrolmen in through the back doors of The Round Table. Some were inconsolable, staring numbly into the shadows of mourners hunched over their beverages, until Gwen placed a brimming glass in their hands and ushered them too into a quiet corner. Others on the force, more hardened by their occupation, jittered, rocking on heels and chattering their teeth, unable to conceal the prevalent worry over the possibility of not receiving further payola from Arthur's operations. But no matter how they appeared, Officer La Paie summed up everyone's feelings this morning when he quipped, "His spirit will live on…in more ways than one". As La Paie's toasted mug slammed onto the tabletop, James heard an ethereal bellow resonate clearly in his mind, forcing him to smile his appreciation of the tribute too.

The police had quickly let James go after some preliminary questioning at the Sourpuss estate. If they had not been introduced, the lawmen had at least seen James in close company with the King as they toured Arthur's various drinking establishments this past week. And if there had been any doubts regarding James' loyalty, they were quickly silenced by the fact that James had held the dying man in his arms, weeping over his still impressive figure, long after the breath had left his body and the police had arrived on the scene.

James' initial shock eccentrically came back for an encore as he noticed a second bullet lodged in the floor, at the very spot where he himself had been standing before his valiant dive to save the punch. In the ensuing confusion, he hadn't just been prey to that much less fun counterpart to drunken vision, the sober phenomenon of hearing double. There had in fact been two shots fired. This confirmed his suspicions, not only about the events of the so-called party, but also as to what happens when people don't drink – he gets shot at. A death knell rang out over the city and James raised his glass to his lips, the question plaguing him – back there, in the dark, had both bullets been meant for King Arthur? Or was one intended for James himself? His morning beer had never tasted so cold.

The table in front of James was covered in empty jugs, decanters, tankards, and flagons. The restaurant out front was closed for the day, as it seemed was half of Cleveland, its citizens nearly all dressed in black out of respect for the dead. After recovering as much as he could from the news, Mitch had driven a dejected Vagabond to The Round Table, picking up Gwen from The Shining Armory along the way. Gwen listened as James recounted the tale over much needed multiple pints; veritably quadruple fisting, both Gwen's hands with mugs at the ready reaching James' lips before his saliva separated him from the glasses he was holding. The two found fifteen minutes of sleep before they heard the secret knock begin its pounding on the back door. Arthur's many friends began to pour in and as James repeated his first-hand account of the murder, Gwen busied herself serving beverages to all the bereaved, leaving the bar open for anyone not crying in their beer to pull their own pints and mix their own cocktails, as Arthur would surely have wanted. James noticed Moonbeam Jim nobly stepping in to down an overflowing screwdriver to which a grief-stricken man could not stop his shaking hand adding tonic. Cinnamon and Sugar walked this crushed soul over to a scat while Gwen brought over a more sensible drink. Over in a shadowy corner, the Mark Maker cousins and their usual entourage of beautiful women were barely visible behind the red tips of their cigars. When more help arrived, Gwen found time to slip into a mourning outfit – French maid with black veil. James considered this too as what Arthur would've wanted.

Candles guttered through the gloom, the crowded space silent with brooding. James glanced up straight into Gwen's plentiful cleavage as she thrust another Excalibur in front of him. Even with his

Service training, James could not crack the mystery of what was in these things. In his mind's eye, he saw Arthur, now at the great bar in the sky, looking down with a perfect view of Gwen's bust, and for the first time being able to fathom the ingredients of her monstrously potent concoctions. And so passed the long hours of the day. Evening fell, visible in this shuttered back room only by the clock's sad face. With ample supplies stashed between her accommodating breasts, Gwen now set about replacing the tabletop candles.

"Thought I'd find you here."

James looked up, startled by the vision of red in front of him. A claret leather body suit within a coat of the same colour - and who knew what other treasures were to be found within its enchanting folds – hung down over strong, athletic thighs to meet obsidian boots at the knees. James immediately identified them as steel-toed but found himself unwittingly frowning at the lack of spurs on the heels, as if this fantasy come to life had raced too far ahead of itself. An invisible finger seemed to raise his chin to gasp and gaze at the most beautiful face he'd ever beheld. Its alabaster a heart framed by strands of auburn hanging down over generous breasts that then looped up to encircle the nipples. Her crimson lipstick perfectly complemented her pale skin, which when she blushed must be divine. This magnificent woman looked incredibly familiar to James and yet he knew that he did not, could not, know her.

Before he could respond to her greeting, elegant fingers clasped his drinking hand and he was stunned to feel a bottle cap press into his knuckles. "I'm so sorry to hear about Arthur," she offered consolingly before letting go and taking the seat opposite him. Edging her chair close enough to his so that her steel toes tickled the collection of grime surrounding James' dirty digits, she began to speak in conspiratorial tones.

"My name's Cherry," she whispered, her lips lasciviously close to his ears. "Cherry Waters. I believe you know my sister Bubbles."

Of course! James mentally smacked his forehead, his body still too shocked to actually move. She looks exactly like Bubbles, though Bubbles surely must've changed her surname. Bubbles, despite the bathing associations of her appellation, happened to be James' favourite performer at Off The Rocks. A smile began to break his momentary paralysis as he recalled what he and Bubbles used to get up to – that time in the public urinal in Soho Square, the night spent in the bathtub emporium on Holloway Road with, mercifully, the water mains shut off, the ingeniously fun way of picking vegetables at her allotment…James' dreamy eyes caught the look of concern on Cherry's face, her serious stare having him half-suspecting telepathy. James threw back the remainder of his Excalibur, knowing he must pay attention to learn how this fiery lady had traveled back in time and found him here. But even if she could read his mind, before he left this particular fancy, he lingered a moment to remember that Bubbles had a tattoo of her namesake rising out of her nether regions up along her hips and insisted to himself that he must make absolutely sure this rose in front of him was not after all Bubbles in disguise.

"Are you quite through?" Cherry inquired. James nodded, wiping the drool off his chin, and sat up to adjust the tension in his lap. "Good. It appears we have been tricked. Triple-crossed to be exact. We weren't the only ones Professor Welles sold a time machine to."

James rapidly shook his head back and forth, wrinkling his brow and rubbing it with his beer mug. His mission kept on getting more bizarre. "What? How?" was all he could mutter in dismay.

"There were three gargantuan, and I mean truly astounding, offers for the machine. 20/20 even used the term 'liver-defying'. Welles accepted them all. He now possesses – somewhere, we still haven't managed to find it – the largest supply of alcohol ever known to man. We've got men looking for it but, the truth of the matter is, it's his. He fulfilled his half of the bargain. It is strange that we haven't been able to locate it. Our satellite investigations have turned up nothing, same with our excavation teams out digging. He must have it stashed all over the globe."

"And the professor himself?" James queried, fearing the worst.

"No sign of him. Disappeared before you even went back in time. The last confirmed sighting came in the night the Queen Bea sailed. He completely broke down in a bar in Tooting Bec, smashed up the entire place. As they carried him off to the mental institution, he was heard to be shouting something about 'perfecting the time machine to transport alcohol' and 'drinking forever'. This only seemed to confirm the suspicions of insanity. Somehow he escaped the next morning and we haven't been able to track him down since. Reports began to come in almost daily, with a strange simultaneousness. The good professor was spotted wearing a beaver skin cap in Berlin, Connecticut while also seen at the same time writhing naked on a bearskin rug in Berlin, Germany. One anonymous tip had spied him beatboxing as a busker in Bakersfield, Nottingham and a concurrent sighting placed him downing copious amounts of borscht in Bakersfield, California. More witnesses than I care to say have put him in a bikini in French coastal Brest, while just as many accounts have a man of his description beaming in strip bars all over Brest, Belarus. But none of these have ever been verified. He could *be* anywhere!"

Cherry placed a pack of Zippers on the table and smiled. James reached for one immediately. The nicotine and sight of smoke between Cherry's lips helped him to relax and concentrate. There were so many questions but one seemed the most logical to get out of the way first.

"So how did you get here?"

"D told you about the American firm who wanted to keep Prohibition intact but change the wording of the Amendment so that they could still manufacture and export the stuff?"

James nodded, although he had forgotten this detail until now. Cherry continued, "It seems they stole the idea from the Canadians." She lowered her voice further. "In the era where we now find ourselves, certain Canadian provinces, Ontario for instance, banned the retail sale of alcohol like they're doing here but the federal government still approved and licensed breweries and distilleries. That way alcohol could carry on being manufactured, distributed, and exported. This firm offered Professor Welles the highest bid, nearly three times our offer, and it seems they got two time machines out of it. Our intelligence discovered their plan was to come back and eliminate you before going back even further and changing the wording of the Amendment. Figured you would be the hard part."

James shifted in his seat.

"That's who killed your friend last night. Man by the name of Johnson. Unfortunately, I have no idea where he is now. I managed to get to his partner though, before that one could even use his time machine..."

"What's his name?"

Cherry looked at Vagabond quizzically, cocking her head to one side. She paused to light another cigarette. "His name was also Jonson. But without the 'h'."

"L-l-l-ike the detectives in the Tintin books?" James asked incredulously, now perched on the edge of his chair in alarm.

Cherry scrunched up her nose. "Well, yes, I guess if that helps you, but let's try and stay on track here. I took this other Jonson out just as he was getting into his machine – it was no easy task finding him, let me tell you – then I hopped in myself and set the controls for three days ago. We knew you were heading for Ohio. I was actually down in Cambridge when I saw the headlines about what happened last night, so I took a chance you might be in Cleveland. And here I am." Cherry smiled. "Just to be safe, I destroyed the time machine when I got here, so we're going to have to squeeze on the way back." James' eyes nearly popped out of his head at the thought.

"Oh, and Foxy got in touch with us. The poor girl was in hysterics because she forgot to give you Ted Williams' coin collection. I went and picked up all the ones from 1918 and before, some paper money too. Worth their original value here but any little bit helps. Foxy was very appreciative. Said she simply couldn't stand to think of you spending a sober night alone." The thought of the skimpy outfit Foxy would be clad in whilst crying over him was almost enough to make Vagabond get up and race back to the future to go comfort her. French inhaling, Cherry smiled through the smoke and fixed James' eye. "She's quite a girl."

James' drinking arm halted halfway to his mouth. A full awkward minute passed in rabid imaginings before Cherry tapped his elbow to help him along.

As if reading James' thoughts, Cherry added, "If we do run into any financial trouble, I've always got this." She slipped a platinum band onto her left ring finger, a diamond glittering amongst ornate Art Nouveau vinework. "But my fiancé will sure be upset if it comes to that."

James felt his spirits dash on the rocks. This was the pits. Cherry, even if she was telepathic, could not fully know what wild fire roared in James' loins for her. Service women, despite their often bouncy exteriors, were tough as nails, deeply committed to whatever cause they gave their hearts. If Cherry was indeed engaged to be married, there was certainly no way she'd sleep with James unless it would somehow advance the mission. And since they were both on the same side... He considered that perhaps the only way to win Cherry over would be to save the world in such a spectacular fashion that she'd be forced to recognise James was the man for her, love and lust blossoming over and over deep in her breast every time anyone anywhere took a sip of a cocktail, their beloved ingredients now finally safe from harm. James noticed his Excalibur glass was surprisingly half-full.

Nevertheless, Gwen came by with a fresh round of four brimming beverages. "Thank you, Gwen, dear." Cherry smiled and turned to James. "We met earlier." Was there a hint in Cherry's eyes of further foxy antics? But another thought was pressing on James' pickled cerebral cortex and he pushed all plans of how to get Cherry out of all that red leather out of his mind.

"You said we were triple-crossed. Surely the Johnsons getting two time machines doesn't count twice?"

Cherry lowered her gaze, lost in the depths of her glass, and sat silent for a moment. "Yes. Yes, you're correct. There is someone else back in time. Working towards the same ends as the Johnsons. Only we have no idea where he is." Cherry broke off and shuddered.

"Who is it?" James gulped, owl-eyed with fear.

"Who knows?" Cherry replied, a chill sweeping through the room, frosting tumblers, shakers, mugs, cocktail umbrellas, tips of noses and other bodily protrusions. James' hand froze to his glass. Icy paralysis set in for a duration in which it seemed several consecutive vats of Vine-Glo could ferment, be emptied, and subsequent hangovers recovered from. Summoning a reserve of strength from an untapped reservoir he was unaware he had, James gulped again, nearly swallowing his teeth, lips, and lower jaw in the process.

"Doctor…Hoo-Nose?"

Dr. Hoo-Nose being the greatest agent of all time, of any Service known to man. Except that he didn't work for any particular Service and any information pertaining to him is obscure to man at best. Taking on assignments as he pleased, mostly for P.O.P.P.Y., C.O.C.A., and other narcotic upstarts or clandestine stimulus groups; working both sides when their interests coincided, as they often did. Rumours along The Grapevine, DRINKS' intelligence gathering branch, abounded, but facts were far from concrete concerning the mysterious doctor. What sparse data existed was usually hearsay, accompanied by a good deal of nostril spray, as speakers of such were involuntarily prone to the grunts, splutters, and other nasal emphases stemming from an uneasy mixture of fear and disbelief. James recalled his briefing on Hoo-Nose by one Captain O. Penbarrell. It ran:

The only son of Rosi Hoo, of the rumoured roaming Chinese canton of Switzerland (still yet to be discovered), and one Arran E.

Nose, a peddler of prosthetic proboscides in Portsmouth, or perhaps a little ways north of there. The most common story in circulation being that the Doctor's parents met while Rosi was out hunting rhinos with a lasso and Arran was following the confounding calls of an imaginary owl that had been obsessing him for 23 months. Wandering the lowlands of Sumatra one night, they walked smack into each other. The impact effected a cure in Arran, and Miss Hoo, hearing his story, was impressed with the thick skin it must've taken to traverse the world for such a cause. Laughing, Rosi was clearly pleased with what she had caught in her noose, and in turn etiquette beckoned to Arran to ask the lovely Miss Hoo to accompany him in search of a soft drink. Sharing this syrupy bubble-bonanza through bendy straws that kept sliding away from them, the pressure exerted by their steadying hands on the glass (and of course to their minds, other forces) eventually brought their lips together, parting only to say 'I love you' hours later.

Here D had interrupted Penbarrell's soliloquy, the heavily inebriated gentleman having lapsed into waxing romantic, obviously as a defence mechanism against facing the horrors of Hoo-Nose's birth and subsequent, as often referred to amongst Servicemen, 'drought of terror'. Even as a baby, he refused a bottle. This unearthly child was next heard of some 15 years later, studying Dosido under a renegade master, the very meticulous Vyvyan Li, on an unnamed, uncharted island in the East China Sea off the coast of Japan. Known to its inhabitants as Huh, this confounded any interrogative attempts to locate the place. At the end of his training, so local legend goes, Hoo-Nose tore his Master to pieces and destroyed his home before fleeing, leaving only a scorched, blackened island.

Reports next place him arriving in the Amazon en route to an apprenticeship in the great drug laboratories, quickly gaining knowledge and experience enough to ascend high amongst the ranks at the World Headquarters Of Central American Recreational Euphoric Substances. Hoo-Nose supposedly worked alongside such luminaries as brothers Joseph and Rico Kane, Al 'Green' Nelson, whose F.R.A.N.K. machines revolutionised processing time, and the infamous Mort Fiend aka Papa Slumber. Hoo-Nose soon wiped them out too, making off with their treasured secrets and advancing his reputation towards the realms of mythology. Feared and respected by weak-minded men looking to break into the game, Hoo-Nose used this eagerness to help thwart would-be revenge plots, government inquiries, and other nuisances. Under the guise of setting up a secret lair, he simultaneously sent seventeen decoys out to all four corners of the globe. DRINKS and other agencies picked up and decoded messages from such disparate locations as Istanbul, Dakar, Oaxaca, Nepal, Tromsø, Dampier, Ontario, Yerevan, Orlando, and Ulm. Upon investigating, the mangled corpses of these entrepreneurial stooges were each found in large waste receptacles behind prominent perfume shops in their assigned areas. When the black hosiery over their heads was removed, surgical scars hinted at what medical tests would later confirm - each lackey now bore the beak of one of his colleagues. Meanwhile Hoo-Nose, under cover of this wild goose chase, sailed west to establish his nefarious HQ in the Galapagos Islands. Or so it is believed. Stolen satellite photos show what appear to be bumps of twin tunnels leading to a simple structure, isolated and obscured from anything that could remotely be called civilisation, out past old factories and distant tar pits. On closer inspection, knots of bodies, struck down in terror and frozen in poses of running away, litter the heavily overgrown trail. Acting Station Chief Hans Kerr reported to DRINKS that Agent Nariz had boogie-boarded out to the region in the hopes of taking some reconnaissance photos but strong fear would not let him approach the shore and anyway there seemed to be no light by which to snap any shots. And this is where the track marks end.

Cherry nodded slowly, acknowledging their worst fears. "We...we believe it's him. Signals we've intercepted allude to...to the Doctor." Her hand trembled, the ice in her beverage knocking against the glass. James squinted jugwards, had there been ice in it before? Cherry continued. "All known narcotics agencies are working together on this one. It would be in their best interests to stop the manufacture and distribution of alcohol. Prohibition greatly accelerated their business in the States. Without drink, people turned to other forms of intoxication. If Prohibition were to be kept going, opiate and stimulant traffic would be at an all-time high. Hhhoo...the Dah...the Doctor must've arrived impossibly early. Have you noticed how much more difficult it is to get a drink here than you thought it would be?"

James, in all his difficulties in obtaining drinks, had not had time to notice this. Besides, despite alcohol's tendency towards sentimentality, a good agent should be focused on the now. During his next sip, Vagabond reprimanded himself. This was vital information of course relating to the present, something he should've picked up on. Well done, Miss Waters, he silently toasted, well done.

"And it's not a pretty scene back in the future. There have been reports of P.O.P.P.Y. and C.O.C.A. agents massacred in the most gruesome ways imaginable, simply for doubting the possibility of time travel. Same for those too frightened to make the attempt. Remember that to the sober mind, it must truly be a terrifying idea."

Cherry Waters and James Vagabond sat in silence for the remainder of their beverages, the sombre tones of the back room perfectly suited to their unease. Although neither could offer certifiable proof that they had ever encountered Dr. Hoo-Nose, each knew that at one time they had been in his presence. This had been felt more than understood, with a distinct chill piercing down to their souls. James had sensed this during the great Fogger Debacle when traces of low-grade heroin were showing up in certain smoked beers. Seconds before the Bern brewery he was investigating exploded, James explicitly remembered a blur racing across the room and, as he would later describe it, 'the gin froze in my blood'. And that was all.

Gwen brought another round of Excaliburs and James lit a cigarette. He knew that soon he would have to start collecting stubbs off the ground again. All this business of non-second*hand* smoking was spoiling him. Almost afraid to ask, he looked into Cherry's eyes and inquired, "Any other news from home?"

Cherry thought for a moment, a warm glow of deep wisdom and understanding emanating from her features, calming James' troubled heart. "The liquorice gangs are thought to be forming an alliance."

James straightened up in alarm. He squinted, "What?"

"Well, nothing's been verified yet but a number of PERNOD agents were spotted at a health conference near Barfleur. The majority of the seminars there were extolling the benefits of ozone and reiki, but as Sam Bucharest and Anna Cedar were also espied on the premises, we're fairly certain most attendees were O.U.Z.O. and RAKI operatives in disguise. That is, however, all we know at present."

James shrugged. This information meant little to him now; he hoped it would continue to mean little to him. He had been forced to drink great amounts of aniseed-flavoured alcohols in his training days for the Service and, as with Slivowicz and now to a certain degree coriander, he had grown somewhat used to the taste. But liquorice flavour was never something he would consume on his own time. He looked about him; it was getting late. The mourning clientele had begun to pass out in their seats. Cherry noticed this too.

"Where are you staying, James?"

"In the alley out back."

"Is there a big enough bin?"

"No, but it's nice anyway."

Cherry rose to leave. "I'll meet you back here tomorrow."

"Tomorrow's the wake," James noted gloomily.

"We'll get a drink beforehand." Cherry flashed a weary smile. "Goodnight, James."

She walked out the front door and into the night beyond. James Vagabond sat staring into his glass. This was all quite unbelievable. Before he could fathom just how much, Gwen came to see if he would like another Excalibur. She looked exhausted but as another drink was something James could never refuse out of principle, he soothed the situation with "Okay Gwen, but this'll be the last one. And thank you." Gwen delivered the libation with a smile and James polished it off in one breath, bringing the empty glass to the bar on his way out the secret entranceway. He was drunker than he thought and by the time he stumbled into the alleyway he was nearly asleep on his feet.

10 – The Moon Shines Bright

Cherry Waters strolled into the back room of The Round Table at four o'clock the following afternoon sporting an exact copy of the body suit she had worn the day before but in black. A long leather jacket, the shade of deepest night, fell below her knees, obscuring the full implications of the garment encasing her most desirable skin from any 1918 eyes. As she sashayed up to the table where he was sitting, James wondered, not for the first time since her arrival, why D had chosen Cherry specifically to make the journey back in time to rescue James. But he knew the answer. She was an excellent agent. It was readily apparent by the way she carried herself and the amount she drank last night. Cherry's acute assessment and handling of this whole Prohibition business demonstrated her intelligence, and those muscular buttocks, which James was now craning back in his seat to view, gave a good indication of her strength. A physical power of which there were only so many ways James wished to be on the receiving end, and although he wished those ardently, he did not at the moment desire a perversion of such force to teach him a lesson in manners. So before tipping over, he returned his chair to the upright position and waved good afternoon.

"Hello there," Cherry charmingly smiled, producing an unopened pack of Murads.

James signaled to Lance for two more drinks. "Sleep well? Where are you staying anyway?"

After lighting her cigarette, Cherry shook the match, blowing it out at the same time, whilst even more extraneously licking her lips. "You might not know about this side of the Service but I have a note from a certain London Madame who lived back in this time. D took care of getting it written. Sort of a letter of recommendation, if I wanted to work at any of these places in America, or anywhere around the globe even. We still use them nowadays," she wrinkled her nose, "You know what I mean. Anyway, first thing I did even before I came to look for you was getting myself settled at The Red Garter. Told them I was on holiday – vacation - and needed a place to sleep. That I'd probably only use the bed for business if I was running out of money. Mama Overcast said fine by her, just as long as they could have the room when I'm not there. With all we need to do, it should be free enough for them and everything seems to be working out fine. Very sweet bunch of girls."

James Vagabond was intrigued by this system. So fascinated in fact, that he did not once sip his beverage while Cherry was speaking. He plucked a cigarette from the pack and asked as coolly as he could manage, "Can I see this letter?"

Cherry threw back her chestnut hair and laughed. "I had to leave it in the office. For identification purposes should I rip them off or something." She fixed James' eye. "Don't worry, I come highly recommended."

They finished their drinks and joined the rest of the mourners getting ready to set off for the wake. But first there was the mass deodorisation of breath to be taken care of, deemed necessary by Gwen. Large white marble bowls had been lined up on a table near the exit door. Full of mint, onions, garlic, bentonite and charcoal, most patrons stood bemused over these dishes, some tentatively popping contents into their mouths, others simply sobbing over them, whilst a few shrieked after rubbing their already-teary-enough eyes with a handful. The crock of vinegar had had to be removed after an elderly gentleman mistook it for a urinal. Gwen had disclosed to James earlier this afternoon that Arthur's organisation was still trying to decide whether or not they should keep up Miller's teetotal cover. Arthur's wishes had been that his true identity should only be revealed if it were to aid the anti-Prohibition movement. Some in the King's camp had come forward yesterday with the view that exposing these Prohibitionists as the cold-blooded murderers they were would greatly help the cause. But most in Arthur's line of work countered that they couldn't prove this and with everything at stake, it would be best for their operations to remain undercover. Word went round that those who were visibly drunk by four p.m. today should not attend the wake but that corpse and casket would later be brought to Camelot for the drinkers to pay their last respects.

A pungent procession made its way out the front doors of The Round Table, mostly steady on its feet, coming to halt a few city blocks away in front of a large stone building. Cherry pointed above the entranceway to the grey and black sign proclaiming 'Robert Graves' Funeral Home'.

"I wonder if Mr. Graves worried much about choosing a career path."

"He could've been a writer," James quipped, and they followed the others inside.

The room, immaculately decked out in lilies, roses, and snapdragons, all heavenly white and regal purple, was, in keeping with Gwen's mandate, only half-full. The flowers added a certain sweetness to the peculiar bouquet. James could tell from the looks in most attendees' eyes that they were experiencing that odd, rarely known if truth be told, confusion – not yet anxiety or panic – of having been drinking all day and then finding oneself without momentary recourse to alcohol. Not wholly perplexing or unpleasant, carried through by having been drinking all day, but disorientating nonetheless.

Soon Mrs. Amaretto Sourpuss and a few others James recognised from the party made their way through the front door. Mrs. Sourpuss caught sight of James straight away and made a beeline towards him, absent-mindedly tugging down her dress in the cleavage. Upon espying Cherry, Amy Sourpuss halted in her tracks, whatever smile may have been forming quickly scurrying back into its shell, demanding even before saying hello, "And who is this?"

"Pardon me, Amy. And allow me to introduce Miss Cherry Waters."

Mrs. Sourpuss scowled and James continued. "Cherry is also an old friend of the Miller family. She was just on her way to visit Arthur when…when it happened."

"Nice to meet you," Cherry offered and had to force her manicured magenta hand into Sourpuss' brittle palm.

"Oh," was all Amy could say in return. She gave James a look of burning disappointment and made her way to the kneeler in front of the coffin. Her face and bearing showed no expression, causing James to wonder if she felt any remorse, any sorrow whatsoever, for what happened at her party. For what happened to his friend.

After five minutes, Mrs. Amaretto Sourpuss and the rest of her sober entourage made their way towards the exit. Before disappearing into the night, Amy Sourpuss' face brightened, ever so slightly. She scurried back to Vagabond, drawing up close to his ear. "Darling James. I'm giving another soirée in two weeks' time. Leaders from Prohibition In Several States Providing Our Unending Righteousness as well as Prohibition A Nationwide Treasured Service will be there. I'd be delighted if you could attend. I trust this one," her eyes sweeping maliciously towards Cherry, "will be gone by then?"

James nearly choked. "Yes, Amy. I'd be…uh…delighted also. And don't worry about Cherry."

Amy Sourpuss then walked out of the funeral home, which is something most people never thought they would see her do again.

Cherry strolled up to James. "What was all that about?"

"I don't know. But it just might help us." James proceeded to fill Cherry in on the details of the first Sourpuss function, or dys- as it were, and told her of this new invitation.

"Let me guess, I'm not allowed anywhere near the front door?"

"Would you want to be? With all those dry horrors inside?"

Cherry wriggled her nose. "I guess not. But that woman irks me."

"I fear she wants to irk me," James shuddered. "But there must be a way we can use all this to our advantage."

The two far-from-home agents from the future stood considering the situation for a while but the time soon came to remove the casket to Camelot. James was glad to have stayed the entire duration of the wake, even if it meant foregoing a drink for a few hours. The afternoon of Arthur's booze buoyed James' bloodstream through the trying evening. He had been a dear friend. And to those looking from the outside in, this did much to establish James and Cherry's credibility as long time associates of the King.

James and Cherry helped to carry Arthur's body to the waiting cabs out back. Unfortunately, after many unsuccessful attempts, the coffin was found to be too large for any of the cars present.

"We'll have to steal a hearse."

"Her what?"

"He won't fit on a horse."

Everyone was on edge from not having had a drink in quite some time. Complicated by the knowledge that a hearse, unlike every other vehicle present, motor or otherwise, would not be equipped with any liquor. As if receiving divine inspiration, Moonbeam Jim smiled and tapped his blind man's stick to his head, hopping in the driver's seat of the long black ride. But not before unscrewing the top of his cane and pouring himself out a hefty libation.

"Load him up!"

With Arthur soon settled in the back, Moonbeam drove off and a collective sigh of relief was exhaled. A lookout gave the all-clear and the floorboards of the waiting cabs were removed. This was the first time James had witnessed the mythical 'bar beneath your feet'. He nearly fainted with joy. Cherry grabbed two bottles and hopped in a car, patting the seat next to her for James to join. Everyone was soon safe inside Camelot. Except for Moonbeam Jim, who, with his portable container, was dispatched to return the hearse, knowing that with the amount of drinking about to take place, the odds of not smashing up the vehicle later on were not in anyone's favour.

The street outside Camelot was quiet but once through the doors there was the curious air of a coronation. Cherry looked around, enthralled. The corpse held court at the back, lying in state on the King's favourite table, surrounded by a crowd of grievers. James admired the fact that, drunk as they were, they weren't singing. Cherry waved to some of her new friends from The Red Garter, dressed in their best to send Arthur on his way to the great never-ending tap. A raven-haired beauty with dozens of black and gold feathers woven into her piled locks smiled back while nearby a buxom blonde displayed the same in plumage of pink and blue. See-through kimonos, suspender belts, and scanty lace, all iridescent rainbows of libidinous hues, seemed the order of the night. The woman James recognised as Sugar simply wore a crown.

"Two Armored Car Bombs, please," Vagabond hailed to the barkeep. James looked forward to showing off his famous trick, but before he could even reach for his beverage Cherry herself had lit a Murad from the flame and was drinking the whole thing down in one go, cigarette dangling out the righthand corner of her painted mouth as James Vagabond looked on in astonishment. She wiped her sleeve across her lips and cast James a withering look. His glass still remained untouched.

The entire spectrum of King Arthur's concoctions, the specialities from all his various venues, was on offer to his memory this evening. Lady Of The Lakes, White Stags, Kinky Dudleys, even the beguilingly simple Merlin, equal parts Merlot and gin, served in a tall glass staff (the container later made famous accommodating drinks 'by the yard'). James and Cherry sampled them all, several times. So did everyone else.

The evening carried on in a strange brew of sorrow and debauchery. Myriad toasts were raised, splashed, and spilled. Cherry fended off advances from every corner, though tarried awhile in the one where the Maker cousins had situated themselves. Her escape came at a fortuitous cry from Moonbeam Jim.

"Limbo!"

Using his very own hollow blind man's stick, drained already of course, and handing the other end to James Vagabond, with his free hand Moonbeam ushered the enthusiastic bending and gyrating patrons under the cane. Soon the slippery floor became a writhing mass of sliding, soaked bodies, unable to get up or simply not wishing to. Sometime around dawn snores replaced the clamour of pleasure.

"AH!' A scream emanated from the coffin. "We're going to be late!"

The hundred or so persons collapsed about the room in various states of disarray rubbed their eyes before hazily casting them towards the casket. A crown emerged from below the open lid, followed by another head of feathers. A hose was found for bodies and bar, and Gwen had the good sense to reinstitute the breath-freshening bowls. Clothes were located, swapped and reswapped, and an unsteady hungover procession began to make its way to the church. "I don't know how it got here," explained Lance to the hearse driver who had been sent from Robert Graves' Funeral Home to pick up Arthur's body, now residing on the curbside. Lance continued the pantomime of scratching his head while the car drove off, at which point Gwen gently removed the pink silk panty from his forefinger and tucked it into his suit pocket as a handkerchief.

The church, unlike the scene at the funeral home, was packed. The service itself was of an appropriate length for the Camelot casualties to catch up on their sleep. James Vagabond forced himself to stay awake, curious to see if Mrs. Amaretto Sourpuss or any of the other sober socialites would partake of the communion wine. His arduous efforts thwarted by the fact that none of them bothered to attend the ceremony. At the end of the proceedings as the mourners were exiting and making their way to the gravesite, James espied a Mr. Vejvoda sitting joyfully at the organ playing what to James' ears sounded suspiciously like a slowed-down version of 'Roll Out The Barrel'. His eyes carried past the pianist and soon settled on a solitary character hovering over the coffin. The figure was familiar to James although he could not quite place him. In his solemn garb, threadbare at the elbows no doubt from hoisting so many pints to his sad looking mouth, this gentleman wore a different timbre of grief from the rest of the assembly. He looked as if he had been up drinking for weeks over the loss of his friend, not simply the few days it had been. James felt a wave of admiration go out towards this man who just then glanced up and caught James' eye, nodding back his own tenderness towards another one of Arthur's beloved. James immediately recognised this personage as none other than the bootlegger Daniel Jackson, whom Arthur had pointed out on James' very first night in Cleveland, oh so long ago. James appreciated Mr. Jackson's show of devotion towards his friend. Surely if James had lost D or Miss Glassbottle, or even 20/20, he would look much the same about now. James continued to watch as Daniel Jackson bent over the corpse. He appeared to be reaching into the coffin, a doctor performing a delicate operation. Jackson then moved aside as James moved closer to investigate. Two bottles were regally placed, one in each of the King's great hands.

"They were his brands, you see. One whiskey, one gin," Daniel Jackson explained solemnly. "To slake his thirst on his journey across the skies."

James peered closer into the scents of musk, chartreuse, and ginger rising from the lace-filled interior. Some of the ladies had also stuffed presents inside to accompany the King wherever he may roam. Soon Gwen, the Maker cousins, and Moonbeam Jim joined James and Jackson. The six raised the coffin from its catafalque and began the heavy walk to the cemetery.

"James!" Cherry's breathless whisper seared into his ear. Vagabond felt his knees buckle. Oh how he had longed to hear her say his name in such tones! The preacher, having just begun the graveside rites, turned to make sure this bustling bubble of activity would not get out of hand. Cherry's haste to reach James' side was not as nonchalant as she had thought. But this was urgent.

"See that man over there? In the back, by the trees, grey fedora, white band, next to the bearded lady in pirate's garb?"

James nodded his affirmation but was admittedly confused.

"That's Johnson."

James froze. Not only was Cherry not beckoning him to bed, albeit at a seemingly inappropriate time, that husky 'James!' was instead pointing out to him another man. One who intended to annihilate him.

"Stay here. I'll handle this." And before James could reply, Cherry was off.

James fixed his would-be killer's image in his mind as he watched Cherry lead Johnson away from the crowd. The rest of the service was spent trying to get a grip on himself, fighting the failures of fear in order to say a proper final goodbye to the man who had been so kind to him, the patron of all drinkers great and small, his friend Arthur Miller.

Back at The Round Table there was a formal, keeping up appearances, meal for the mourners and when Gwen had ushered the last of the suspiciously sober grievers from the restaurant, she opened the back room with a long sigh of relief. Soon it was much the same scene as the night before at Camelot, minus the dead body.

Presently Cherry came bursting through the doors, immediately sighting James and pulling him to her side. "Don't worry," she assured him with a wink, "he was driven off asleep."

110

James swallowed, pausing a moment to steady himself. "So what happened?"

"We went for a ride in the hearse."

Confusion rattled James' brain. "But it was parked behind the trees the whole time!"

Cherry smiled, blushing slightly. "I still can't get used to driving on the wrong side over here." She turned away to join the others. "Let's hope next time I can get him in that hearse for good."

As she sauntered into the crowd, James – breath attuned to the swivel of her hips – meditated on Cherry's words. She had done well. Eliminating Johnson completely had been out of the question, he considered. Avenging a dear friend's murder by slaying his assassin at said friend's own funeral is too good, and complex, an idea to come true. Almost impossible to put into practice at such short notice. James finished his drink and set off in search of another one.

A plethora of reporters seemed to be hanging about The Round Table this evening. Most had left after having their fill of the free food but a few stayed on to partake of the festivities in the back room. Even now some earlier departees were returning. James recognised a few faces from the past week's drinking binges. However, it was only today that he noticed they might be journalists as they scribbled furiously throughout the funeral.

"Gwen, those men over there, the ones with the notepads. Do they write for the papers?" James asked with some concern.

"Indeed they do, Sir James, indeed they do." Gwen placed a reassuring hand on his arm. "But have no fear. Not a single one of them would dream of betraying Arthur's true identity. In fact, while you were getting reacquainted with Miss Cherry, we had a meeting with the relevant editors and writers about what the public should and should not be told about the Miller organisation's activities. And everyone has stuck to the story. Mighty noble of them. After all, being unbiased gentlemen of the press, they can't technically be on the payroll. But what's a free meal here or glass of beer there? After all, drinks are given away free with meals anyway." Gwen giggled, tipsily.

At the bar, James spotted a forlorn Daniel Jackson staring so deep into his glass it might be a telescope to China. The two men nodded at one another betwixt lengthy sips for the better part of an hour. James was greatly impressed by this man, who was setting the pace of their drinking by always finishing a good slug or two ahead of Vagabond. Valiantly James strove to sup faster and faster until a look of admiration seemed to broach Jackson's dark brow. At long last James considered it might be appropriate to engage in conversation. He queried the rumour he had overheard a few times that day.

"I understand you'll be taking over as head of operations?"

Daniel Jackson looked Vagabond dead in the eye. "It has fallen to me, yes. And I will continue the good fight in the name of our dear departed friend."

After another protracted silence, Daniel continued. "From what I gathered from Miller, he intended to show you more of how we work this week. Would you mind meeting me tomorrow? If you're not too busy that is. More than ever, we need a solid course of action." Jackson jotted down an address on a cocktail napkin and slid it along the bar to James.

"Of course, Mr. Jackson, of course. Shall we say 3 p.m.?"

It was agreed and the two continued to drink, and talk occasionally in the midst of long periods of quietude, sometimes discussing various brewing or distilling techniques, conjecturing what the days ahead might hold, and often making lists of animals they were unsure could drive an automobile and debating the finer points thereof. Towards dawn, Cherry walked by with some of her new friends from The Red Garter. She blew James a kiss as they headed out the door.

Back in the alleyway, waiting for sleep to come, James struggled to focus on the two sparkling moons above, their dance approaching the erotic whenever he hiccupped. Try as he might, James could not bring them together into one single sphere. As his vision began to spiral off towards the realms of sleep, spinning faster and faster as he neared total blackout, a bright light began to shine, emanating from the intersection of the Venn diagram those heavenly bodies presented. Dazzled, for one split second before unconsciousness, James glimpsed the primordial spark of a plan.

11 - Poppycock Tales

"Tea?"

"What's it really?"

"New batch of whiskey I'm working on. But go on, take a whiff."

Vagabond eyed the teacup Daniel Jackson, ever the conscientious host, was offering him at precisely four o'clock. James took the mug in his hands, hesitantly moving it up to his nostrils.

"How did you do that?" he queried.

Jackson clapped James on the shoulder. "Arthur told me about your teapot suggestion. I must say I found it inspired. Went and asked my man Evan Scent to stir something up for us. Very clever chemist he is, works wonders. Right now he's tackling the bouquet of when we want it to appear milky."

James raised an eyebrow.

Jackson stated, "Simply add Pernod."

This was now the third day in a row James Vagabond had spent touring the fermenting factories with Daniel Jackson, now head of the vast empire of vats Arthur Miller had situated about Cleveland. Day One had taken them to three covert breweries. There were more on the agenda, with Daniel anxious for Vagabond to visit them, but James felt an almost filial connection to the silos of suds at first sight and had to be dragged out the doors of the first two. His resistance only conquered by the promise of more beer. But the third proved too enticing. In fact he spent the night on the floor of this last site with his arms wrapped about a barrel, lips nuzzling the tap in perfect contentment. The next day was more trying. Smaller venues taking in various backstairs bathtubs, surreptitious radiator set-ups, and grape-stained sinks. It was at one of these furtive laboratories that James had the opportunity to sample Vine-Glo past its due date. And although he much preferred it to the non-alcoholic version from the Sourpuss estate, he was glad whiskey was on the menu today.

James was greatly impressed by the range of operations the Miller organisation had in place and with the care taken to conceal them. "It had been no mean feat closing down a lifetime's worth of work and then starting everything up again underground. All while scrambling to secure respectable-seeming jobs and making sure all the old breweries and such appeared to stay out-of-use. Couldn't salvage much from them without the authorities suspecting. Still don't know what happened exactly. Politicians had a sudden change of heart...to no heart at all. It was like an icy wind hit Cleveland, hell, all of Ohio. And it still doth blow."

Here James gulped, itself suspicious without a cup to his lips. He hoisted the tea-scented whiskey. Cherry's deductions concerning Johnson, Hoo-Nose, and how it was so much harder to get a drink here than one had anticipated were all on the money. This wasn't how James had been briefed it would be.

Setting aside his emptied cup, Vagabond cast his eyes over his new surroundings. About this large cement warehouse sat a dozen motor vehicles – black Model T's, cream-coloured Winton Tourings, two sky blue Milburn Coupes, a petite green Templar Four - in various states of disrepair. Red-faced men in greasy overalls strode about to perch under hoods, clanking inside purposefully. The rhythm of the wrenches reminded James of a distant Dutch tune. Hanging heavy in the air was the tang of oil, sweat, exhaust, and the curious smoothness of sandalwood.

After exchanging a few quick words with Daniel Jackson, Mike the foreman gave five quick rings to a nearby bell. The mechanics hurried to the high windows. Scanning the streets outside, they presently gave the all-clear, staying put to continue their vigil as Daniel deftly carried a ladder to a vent in the far corner of the ceiling. Once he and James had scrambled inside the ventilator shaft, Daniel motioned back to the garage and explained, "It's good cover for what you're about to see."

James nodded his approval but remained perplexed. Casting a rare smile back at James, Daniel began to crawl ahead to a drop in the metal tube. Descending the steps they found there, Daniel whispered, "We're inside the wall now." They climbed down further than they had traveled up to reach the vent and all became clear to James as his feet hit the ground and fragrant potent whiskey fumes caressed his nose. He inhaled luxuriously, eyeing Jackson doing the same. Daniel explained, "We have to take care to keep the upstairs filled with other, stronger aromas."

Pride filled James Vagabond as he peered about the basement in which they now found themselves. James felt honoured to know such accomplices and genuine gratitude for the privilege. Daniel must've saved the best for last, for scattered about this subterranean hideaway were gigantic containers of whiskey distilling its grains out. Looking about him, James saw there was no other entrance or exit to this underground paradise than the way they had come. Daniel handed him an open-topped ceramic teapot, similar to the one Jackson was himself now plunging into one of the vats.

"We can't stay long, James. You wouldn't think it but these vapours can do some serious damage. We have to keep this area heavily ventilated, flues and pipes all over the place. More orifices than a man reasonably knows what to do with." Daniel gestured about them. "At night the camouflaged fans on the roof take over."

Marveling at the inventiveness of his cohorts, James inspected the walls but could see nothing that would allow the room to breathe. Daniel continued, "But I wanted to talk to you about something first."

Vagabond submerged his teapot in the vat and drank deep.

"What is it, Daniel?" he asked solemnly.

"Want you to go on a little mission for me. Take that lovely lady of yours if you like. Can't say for certain whether there'll be any danger involved, most likely no, but you two can handle yourselves whatever comes up. Heck, Moonbeam Jim can see that. I need a locale on the other side of town scoped out. The Red Dragon, a speakeasy. Not like they aren't all now... We don't have much to do with the place besides supplying their gin. Haven't been there myself in a long time, especially with all the commotion. But I'm getting reports that lately people just aren't having the same type of good time there they used to. Not sure what's going on, deliverymen can't glean much. But that's what you're going to tell me. You'll need the password to get in. I'll send that along later this evening, changes weekly. What do you say, James?"

The fresh air smacked James in the face as he stumbled out into the street after having agreed to scout for Daniel Jackson that night. Jackson stayed behind to talk to Foreman Mike and the mechanics about further hidden bottle compartments to be added to the Templar Four. The pleasant breeze revived a James Vagabond who was well on his way to nodding off on his feet, so effective had those fumes been. Had he not loved the physical act of drinking so much, James would've thought intoxication-through-inhalation was the way to do it. After rounding a few corners, he paused to catch his breath, steadying himself with a hand on the wall of a tavern-cum-restaurant. Gazing through his fingers, with his head falling every which way in an attempt to focus, he finally made out the words "Prohibition SNOhibition!" barely covered by a new coat of grey. As his eyes drooped again, they caught a horrifying scene painted below this valiant battle cry. A blizzard poured out of two whiskey bottles high in the sky over what appeared to be a post-apocalyptic Cleveland. The snow wrapped around decaying bodies and skeletons obviously frozen from a lack of anything suitable to drink, attested to by the hideous grimaces on longing faces. After some consideration he belched his approval of this nameless hooligan's message and concluded it would be best to lie down before tonight's important mission. Sleep, the stout black flow of sleep, that was what he needed. Another refreshing draft streamed by, sparking in his memory something to do with slumber, with dreams and nocturnal visions. Now what was it?

Soon Vagabond found himself in front of The Red Garter. He hiccupped his recognition, remembering he meant to invite Cherry along for the evening's reconnaissance work. Stumbling up the steps, he fell face first into the entranceway, his red nose ringing the doorbell. James shook himself into shape. Such sloppy carriage was not befitting one of his elite drinking stature. But it was more than just drinking, such airy spirits were a mighty force to be reckoned with. Madame Overcast amusedly made her way to the door, having been watching the whole spectacle from her seat in the main room. As Mama Overcast drew back the curtain, Vagabond sensed in her smile that he had been seen. Already struggling to keep steady on his two feet, he could not completely hide his agitation that someone, anyone, let alone Cherry and Arthur's confidante, might think he couldn't handle his liquor. He took a deep breath as the door opened, sliding as much as he could into his usual calm composure. "I'm a friend of Cherry's."

"Of course you are, dear," grinned Mama Overcast and she led him by the hand up to Cherry's room.

Cherry Waters lay asleep on her bed. Flames tangoed atop double-wicked red candles dripping wax all over the chest at the foot of her bed. The walls were decked out in carmine satin, with whips and chains guarding the windows. Sheets of cadmium silk curved over Cherry's slinky body, her auburn locks nestled into a sleek silver pillow. The scents of Tibetan Tantric ritual incense drifted in from unknown quarters. Such a potent breeze knocked James flat on his arse.

Cherry sleepily opened her eyes at the thud and smiled. James sat up, dizzily recounting what Jackson had told him. Yawning, Cherry turned on her side and mumbled "Okay, but I'm going back to sleep now" with tantalising smacks of her lips. James scrambled to his feet, immediately collapsing again on the bed next to her. Spinning, spinning, spinning, he descended through layer after layer of splendiferous flashing lights.

Some hours later they awoke in the spoon position. Cherry grinned enigmatically over her shoulder. "James?"

"Yes?"

"Didn't Arthur take your gun away?" And with that she hopped out of bed. "C'mon, we've other more pressing issues to attend to."

After a long walk, they arrived in front of a large, abandoned-looking cement building, somewhat similar to the auto-repair-shop-cum-distillery James had been in earlier that day. Jackson had warned them against taking a cab so as to not arouse suspicion. Cherry verified the address of this unmarked establishment by checking the shop numbers to the left and to the right, each with a large alleyway in between; James scouting these passages for a possible place to sleep later that night. When Cherry returned and nodded her confirmation, they approached the rusted red door and knocked the required three quick three long and three quick raps. After thirty tense seconds, an invisible panel slid back at eye level and a voice boomed out of the darkness, "Who goes there?"

"Arnold 'Eggs' Benedict", James declared with confidence, his hands at his sides adding air quotes to 'eggs'. If this action was noticed, it went unremarked upon.

"And the lady?"

Cherry curtseyed, again extraneously, and announced herself, "Roseanne Barleycorn."

"You may enter The Dragon."

The sounds of oxidised locks twisting preceded a slow creak of the door as it opened. A man in a court jester's outfit complete with fishnet stockings and holding a battered shield greeted them. "An honour to have her Ladyship grace us with her presence this evening." Cherry curtseyed again. The jester continued, "Follow me, if you will" and the three set off down the long dark corridor at the end of which was a door with a double-headed red dragon painted on it. The creature was terrifying and confusing, and terrifying in its confusion. One face appeared sleepy, dreaming, a glazed-over eyeball searching the heavens, whilst the other – at an impossible angle to the first – perplexedly viewed the scorched ground as if, were it not about to shut in slumber, would surely be going berserk. The second head reared above the first in a frenzy, jaws open as if to devour its partner. James noted its wings contorted into the semaphore for 'X', thus marking the spot. Pausing to adjust his fishnets, the court jester opened the door for them before ambling back to his post.

James and Cherry descended into the darkness and noise below. The somewhat slippery steps of the circular staircase led into the corner of a large room, its walls all painted black. About these panels were depicted the dual-noggined guardian of the entryway, dueling with itself in a variety of outlandish poses – whilst attempting to seduce a cow to the horror of an old woman (dated Chicago, October 8, 1871); fleeing the White House on August 24, 1814; two further portraits of this deranged majestic beast snooping around the U.S. Patent Offices. The multitudinous shadows of the place surely covered even more than the grime James and Cherry sensed about them. They made their way through the thick blue smoke to the bar. Seating themselves at the only two free stools, they signaled to the bartender. This blond mustachioed man, in a white shirt with black vest and a tie bearing the emblem from the front door, soon made his way over. Cleaning a glass in his hands, he eyed the strangers suspiciously. "Vat can I get you folks?"

"Two Red Dragon's Eyes, please".

"Very goot."

The two shots arrived bubbling like sulphuric geysers. Cherry and James threw them back and licked their lips, each mentally calculating the contents of this delicious and extremely potent concoction. Cherry signaled for two more, then another additional two, and the bartender, seeming to relax a little, complied. Turning on their stools, Vagabond and Waters surveyed the scene. It was much like Daniel Jackson had described – pockets of animated conversation punctuated by sleepy souls sitting slumped on their own.

Presently, a large bearded fellow stood up from one of the groups, wrapped his bear-like arms around two cohorts, and the three bounded up to the bar, gesticulating wildly to the barkeep. James wondered what sort of drinks they could possibly be ordering. The bartender sniffed and set about making them.

"So there I was, the Hercules of 1917..." the bearded man shouted.

"Mmm-hmm, Mmm-hmm..." one companion nodded along at a frantic tempo while the other let out a lengthy exhalation, his eyes wide and wild in pure amazement.

Cherry and James inclined their heads to catch more of the lightning-quick staccato dialogue.

"It's got like-"

"Sure, sure-"

"Yeah, yeah-"

"Of course, you know-"

"And bats, don't forget the bats..."

"Who could?"

"But it's like that boat you have-"

"The one with the-"

"That she-?"

"No, no, the other one-"

"With all the sperm whales?"

The bearded man smacked the speaker, fixing him with a beady stare. He turned to his other friend and solemnly informed him "You best get your boats in order." The three took their newly arrived beverages, bouncing, jostling, and jumping back to their seats.

Cherry and James glanced at each other in wonderment. Scanning the room saw similar rapidly-paced conferences of confidence. In the middle distance, a man lost in reverie nodded forward, his monocle dropping into his barely touched beverage. Cherry couldn't help but smile at this. Another solitary figure spun his head around and around at an impossibly slow speed. Occasionally the lines of his face would twist as he strained to hear an incantation emanating from an invisible tiny speaker sat atop his nose. After watching a man watch his own cigarette burn out on his lips, Cherry turned to Vagabond. "I'm still worried about Johnson. Mitch drove him quite aways away, in fact he just returned late this morning, but no doubt Johnson'll be hightailing it back here soon and we're going to have to take care of him."

James paused to consider but before he could reply, Cherry nodded to the bartender ambling towards them, despite the fact that each had full drinks in their hands. The man leant forward over the bar and asked in low tones, "Vould you folks care to sample the new specialties of the house?"

Cherry rubbed James' leg with hers for a second and James gulped heavily as she asked, 'And what might those be?"

The barkeep smiled. "Ah, you are British. The gentleman as vell?"

James nodded.

"Very goot. I too come from a distant shore. The name is Mickey. Last October my vife Anna and I set sail from our home in

Helsinki…to land in this sink of Hell. Capricious, I think is the vord, she's long gone now. And as if to pour salt in my drinks, this new recipe has just arrived from Brazil – cachaça, sugar, and lime. The Caipirinha, they're calling it. Of course ve spice it up. Along those lines I can also offer you gen-u-vine coca cola." He winked, sadly, before picking up a towel and glass and setting about cleaning it. "And there's the laudanum. Vich has kept me company on many a lonely night."

"Laudanum?" James asked, a little too loudly.

Mickey cast a bittersweet smile. "Yes. It's like an opium vine."

"I know what it is." James cooled his voice down. "But, say, I've not seen it around these parts before."

Mickey, pleased to have engaged their interest, explained. "Gentleman came in the other day, or veeks ago, who knows, difficult to keep track of time ven you never see the sun. Set up our connection, for this and the coca leaf." He nodded towards the bearded man. "Business has been booming. Some have even abandoned the drink to further dive into these indulgences-" The look of horror on James' face gave Mickey pause. He cleared his throat. "Though of course a few of our old regulars stick to their beloved visky. And everybody else is mixing it up and having a very high ball indeed."

"It's funny," Mickey continued, "I've never seen that man since, but the stock keeps on arriving, uncannily punctual in suiting our needs. And shortly after that one and only visit, another character valtzed through the doors, ex-military, had the air of a black marketeer about him. Even gave his name, 'Adam Pause' or something like that. He vas mighty convincing and gave us a very good deal on some oxygen generators that may or may not have fallen off a Fokker D.VII recently. Explained that if every hour the smokers took a hit off the old gas, it vould provide a much more pleasurable experience. Along the same lines of downing a glass of vater every three drinks, stays avay the dehydration. Great in theory but a pain in the Arzberg to get any of these opium fiends to comply."

A shy-looking man in a raccoon cap appeared next to Cherry. "I'll have a laudanum here, please."

"Vould you care for sugar with that?"

"Why yes, of course."

Mickey departed to fetch the man's order. Replaying the bartender's words in her head, Cherry placed her hand on James' shoulder and felt his entire body stiffen underneath her fingers as he too realised what she was thinking.

"It's why we haven't seen him yet, isn't it?"

"You think he's been back...setting things up?"

"P.O.P.P.Y. and C.O.C.A. have extensive records of the drug operations dating back hundreds if not thousands of years. Hoo Nnnn- the Doctor would have access to all that. It's just a matter of being here and moving the pieces around."

Vagabond clenched his eyes shut and shuddered. Once more he begrudgingly felt a wave of respect pass through him. Recognition of his enemy's evil genius and that clear-headed thinking that is the result of abstaining from the very vices one's Service thrives on and protects. Automatically James signaled for more drinks. Mickey held up two fingers and James shot back four. Then he put up his other hand to indicate six. Presently, lime wedges now bifurcated upon their rims, a half dozen Red Dragon's Eyes in martini glasses appeared in front of James and Cherry. Finding themselves in the midst of the legendary Doctor's operations, they were going to need these and more.

"Once...there was a time..." Cherry began, resolve showing in her eyes. "...I was delivering a litre of fermented panda's milk to the Convivial Connoisseur's address in Amsterdam. I...I saw him

124

then. Or at least I can't shake the feeling that I did. It happened as if in a dream and to this day I cannot say for sure it wasn't real. But he was determined, at any cost, to snatch and replace the bottle with one of his own. Panda's milk laced with China White. Just to thwart our operation. That laughter…it was…it was unbearable."

James placed a comforting hand over hers. Cherry smiled but needing no consolation she jerked her arm away. Good thing too, Vagabond thought, that engagement ring was like a dagger through palm, heart, and hips. Suddenly a sonic blast rang out next to James' right ear. A thin man in a cheap dark suit and black homburg had swiped his pint against the brass rail of the bar. Underneath the lingering hum, the man was shouting, great gobs of saliva splashing from his lips at each word.

"But no! No one wants to read fiction nowadays. As if this all wasn't just a fiction-" The speaker swept his arms wide to indicate much more beyond their immediate surroundings, slipping in the process and again banging his glass upon the brass. James looked around to see who this man might be conversing with but the only one paying him any attention was Mickey, awaiting an order.

James Vagabond was delighted. This was the sound of pure, unadulterated alcohol! The man was visibly, unapologetically drunk. Cherry sensed it too and was up procuring a stool for their new friend. Sitting him down, she offered, "May we buy you a drink, sir?"

With glassy eyes, the man glared at her for a full thirty seconds before realising what meaning Cherry's words held. "Oh…oh, yes…sure thing. Thanks very much. That would be a rare delight." He then proceeded to fall off his stool onto the sticky floor below. Cherry and James helped the man to his feet. Once seated again, he shook each of their hands, both left and right, with both his left and right hands.

"Quarterly. Nicholas Quarterly. Proud correspondent of whatever paper decides to pay me."

"So you're a journalist?" Cherry smiled.

"Exactly. And I'll have a gin."

James motioned to Mickey for three gins. Mickey countered with six fingers and James, after roughly calculating how much time they'd be spending with this Nicholas Quarterly, raised three more digits to make nine. Mickey soon placed three trios of glasses on the bar, two-thirds of which containing slices of lime. Nicholas downed two as if quenching a terrible thirst before raising the last towards James and Cherry, holding and sipping the beverage in a regal manner.

"You'll have to forgive me, folks. And thanks for the gin. I've been here since all day. Woke up on the floor right over there in fact and just stayed." He paused to belch, looking much relieved afterwards. "I have an assignment due tomorrow, once again extolling the great effects this sobering up of the nation is bringing about. That's all people want to read nowadays. Accounts of their own moral righteousness staring back up at them. So that's what I have to write. And I can't produce that trash unless I'm damned near blind drunk." He threw back the remainder of his drink and signaled to Mickey for three more. "That's what I was saying about no one reading fiction anymore. Or what they think is fiction. Look around - and doubtless you've been in many a joint like this in our fine city – how can they say the nation is sobering up when the bourbon flows so freely. And of course now there's…" Nicholas touched his nose knowingly, nodding towards the boisterous chatter and pointing at a solitary soul sleeping in his chair. Quarterly winked, with pronounced force and knocked himself off his stool again. He managed to climb back up before Cherry could get to him and continued. "I write novels when I'm not doing this. But people don't want stories anymore, they've become dangerous or passé depending on how you look at it. So I bring home the bacon writing nonsense. Though believe you me, one day there will be bacon-flavoured beer, vodka with bacon in it, bacon with vodka in it, bacon everything. Pigs will fly and rule the world."

James, knowing the man to be quite inebriated, did not question this. Instead he queried, "So you're a novelist?"

"Exactly. More gin please. I've written all these tomes and publishers won't touch them. But sure as hell if I slapped up a manifesto yet again proclaiming the bogus perils of alcohol and took to the public speaking circuit, I'd be a damned millionaire. But listen to this…I've got this one story that's twenty-four hours rejoicing in the life of Cleveland, before these troubles of course, loosely based on the Aeneid. Huh? Pretty good, right? Another where this little girl is obsessed with old man Vladimir. Maybe she should be a vampire, or he, or both. Naw, never catch on. Oh oh one where there's this baseball catcher, you know our national pastime right?" here Quarterly clamped his fists together and swung maniacally, "…anyway a catcher named Ryan Eyre. He goes a little nuts. Locked in an attic for a bit, you know what I'm saying…And my favourite is about this bug who's a traveling salesman, he can fly, you see…oh oh and this rather Utopian story called 'War And Peace Too'." Nicholas paused, quite pleased with himself, and lit one of Cherry's cigarettes.

The Red Dragon appeared to be emptying out. All the men sitting by themselves had long since fallen asleep. The Hercules of 1917 and his cohorts now bounded out the door, on their way to attempt a long – constantly updated and minutely detailed - list of feats of strength. "…I tell you, not like last time when our boy was having trouble reanimating that recently deceased equine…and then we'll be moving on to the pole toss, young Jetski won't know what hit him…" Nicholas continued his alcohol-fueled rant on the nation's ever decreasing selection of acceptable reading material. Slipping and sliding as usual, one of his wild gesticulations brought his head straight into the brass railing, emitting more of a thud than the previous ringing of his pint glass. The collision seemed to awaken a memory within him. Quarterly looked at his watch and jumped up.

"Well I'll be…my apologies, James and Miss Cherry. I've got to hand in 2000 words in an hour. This will be a noble experiment. It was a pleasure meeting you both. We'll have to do this again sometime." And with that he was off, practically flying up the stairs.

"Just like that bug he was talking about," Cherry grinned and picked up her coat, motioning to James that it was time for them to leave also.

12 – Lace Of Spades

"I see," nodded Daniel Jackson, leaning back to reflect and falling straight through a wall. Wood, plaster, and what appeared to be a bat toppled onto his supine body. James helped fish the unaffected Jackson out of the pile of dust, debris, and departing animals in flight, Jackson brushing himself off as if this sort of thing happened all the time. The two were taking 'tea' in the basement of a dilapidated house, though there hadn't been time to locate any teacups or pots so to any outside observer it appeared that they were simply drinking. But James and Daniel knew better, they'd called it 'tea-time' and thus it would be. Besides, no outside observer would dare enter this dank, dark cellar or the disaster-prone environs above.

"Can't understand why anyone would want to taint perfectly good wine with opium, or drink cola in the first place unless there was whiskey in it. But to each their own, James, to each their own. That is, after all, what we're fighting for."

A further beam fell from the ceiling.

"No doubt you noticed the sign reading 'condemned' as we were walking in. Perfect cover. This used to be my home, you know. When all the crazy talk of Prohibition began, I started taking my aggression out on these very walls. By the time the law was passed, half the house was in ruins and I was registered living clear across town. I brought the mess to the attention of the authorities and once they'd declared it unfit for habitation I set up that distillery over there." He nodded to an immaculate collection of brass pipes and copper kettles in the far corner of the room. "No one's ever suspected a thing."

Daniel belched and began rummaging around the wreckage. After a minute, he produced two pint and two shot glasses, blowing off dust and cobwebs and then wiping them with his shirtsleeves. "It's high time I introduced you to the beverage that Mark 'Boiler' Maker bestowed his moniker upon. Or took his name from. I've heard the story many different ways. But in the end, it hardly matters when you taste the sweet bliss of beer and whiskey mixing in your throat."

Jackson turned a spigot to fill the shot glasses with his homemade spirits and emptied two bottles into awaiting pints. With a sense of care and grand enthusiasm he handed a pair to James, who did his best to pretend he wasn't already aware of this ritual from the future. Daniel dropped the smaller container into the larger, swinging it to his lips, and downing the drink all in one go. He let loose a rare smile of extreme pleasure, holding his gaze upon James in anticipation. Vagabond followed suit. When James had wiped his lips and then licked the transferred alcohol off of his hand, he observed, "I can't help noticing that while Arthur had to hold off until 10 PM, you're pretty much drinking from morn until the following morn and back again?"

"Yes." Daniel paused, nodding profoundly. "I see what you're saying. Like you, I count myself amongst the fortunate few." He turned towards the taps. "Another?"

After a second boilermaker, James doing his best not to seem at home with the ceremony, Daniel returned to the business at hand. "The Red Dragon's not the only place in town that's serving opium and cocaine concoctions these days, but I've got an eerie feeling that it's the source for all those other ventures. And if we don't learn what's going on now, our beloved boozers might soon be in for a big shock."

James Vagabond strolled back towards The Round Table, his inner self a curious mixture of contentment from the astronomical quantities of alcohol he and Daniel Jackson had put away and a sense of urgency, heightened by the fact that these freedom fighters still had no clear course of action. With his mind thus engaged, James' heart sent signals of a different order. How wonderful these nights spent with Cherry – gorgeous, stunningly perfect Cherry. How tantalising this mission was, would he ever get closer to her, as close as he desperately desired? And the next thing James knew, a blur of red leather and chestnut hair was flying straight at him.

"James! James!" Cherry threw her arms around him and dragged him into a side street. His instantaneous arousal complicated by the seriousness in her eyes. Perhaps this was true love.

"Johnson's back!"

Cherry smacked James' head upright again after it dropped to gaze at his own groin.

"I went to The Round Table to fetch something for dinner. But before I got to the front door, Lance walked out…with Johnson! I crouched behind a car until he was on his way and then Lance filled me in. Said Johnson had been asking about you, he'd been there yesterday as well, claiming you two were old friends. Wanted to know if anyone had seen you and where you might be staying. Lance didn't let on a thing. Told me it was the worst phony British accent he'd ever heard."

"When did all this happen?"

"Just now. As soon as the coast was clear I came looking for you."

Vagabond exhaled deeply, calming his raging emotions and letting his eyes scan the ground for smokeable cigarette butts. "Well, he's obviously not going back to The Round Table any time soon. And Lance very well wouldn't have shown him the back room. Let's go get you that dinner."

Sitting over a table of sausage and sauerkraut, grapes and gin, James and Cherry reviewed the facts. Lance had felt it would be safer if they ate in the kitchen and the two agents acquiesced.

"...it won't be easy. He may not even know himself who he's working for. But he'll definitely be able, if not willing, to tell us where he's hidden the..." Cherry's eyes darted about the room. "...the machine. And we'd best destroy that soon."

James swirled his glass in front of his eyes, trying to mentally guess how the strands of cabbage that had fallen from his lips into his gin would affect the taste. "People like him are in it for the money. A businessman more than any sort of indulger. I'd bet spirits would eventually make him talk. But I hate tying people up and forcing them to drink. For starters, I don't understand the psychology of not wanting to in the first place. And then it drips out of their mouths or they spit most of it out and I can't stand to see alcohol wasted so. Still, as a businessman, he must have some vices."

"We know those to be gambling and prostitutes. Though he's a crap lay." Cherry threw her head back, laughing. James swallowed the saddest gulp in the world. It was over by the time Cherry's eyes took him in again. She winked. "You leave this to me."

The following evening the man known as Johnson made his routine enquiry regarding James at The Round Table. Lance did as he was instructed and informed Johnson that a man similar to the one Johnson had described – an Englishman at any rate – had been in an hour earlier.

"He complained there was no fish and chips on the menu, insisted our specialties should be spelled with an extra 'i' in the middle, finally settled on sauerkraut and würst, smoked three cigarettes, and then wandered off towards the lake. He did seem a bit depressed." Lance pointed in a direction that would be sure to lead Johnson past The Red Garter.

Meanwhile James Vagabond was well into his fifth hour hiding in an unoccupied room of the cathouse. Daniel Jackson had relayed the message this afternoon that a man fitting Johnson's description had been asking for James at a few of the nearby nightspots. Daniel gave strict instructions that Vagabond was to remain hidden out of sight in The Red Garter until Jackson himself came to pick him up later that night. Upon hearing this command, James looked forward to thoroughly investigating the wide spectrum of blood-racing lingerie and titillating accoutrements on offer, only to learn upon arrival that the girls had removed all such traces of anything that might distract his alertness. Pacing the floorboards and finishing up another bottle of whiskey, he tucked the other three bottles on his person snugly into bed.

On cue, Sinnamon strolled casually out of the side street where she'd been waiting and fell in next to a determined but lost-looking Johnson. A dark mink coat, cut in such a way as to reveal optimal cleavage, was also short enough to show off the fishnet stockingtops her thigh-high black boots did not conceal. She placed her hand in Johnson's pocket and licked his ear lightly as she spoke.

"Looking for a good time, stranger? I know I am."

Johnson froze. Etched upon his face were lines of discouragement and frustration from fruitlessly searching for James Vagabond these past few days. A roll in the hay would surely relieve the tension and he could begin his search anew, refreshed. Sinnamon took his hand and with minimal resistance led him to The Red Garter. Mama Overcast smiled politely as they entered and Sinnamon brought Johnson to a room upstairs. Waiting inside, Spice lay wearing an invisibly thin one-piece lace garment running from neck to toe and displaying everything in between. Johnson was so astonished he barely registered the girls switching places. Spice beckoned him to the bed, removing his coat and shirt, and began to lavishly apply a tangy oil to his back. Massaging him deeply, she responded to his every 'Oh!' with one of her own, until anyone listening outside the room would no longer be able to discern that this was only a massage. After ten minutes she stopped and wiped her hands clean on one of the many scarves lying nearby. Still straddling his back, she reached over and grabbed a deck of cards and pair of handcuffs. Turning Johnson over, Spice dangled the iron rings, the cool metal lightly caressing his skin as she ran it up his chest. She fanned the cards out in front of hers.

"Feeling lucky tonight, big boy?"

Johnson blushed then beamed, "What do you have in mind?"

"A simple cut of the cards," Spice explained, smiling and swinging the manacles in front of his face. "If I win, I get to tie you up and have my way with you." Spice paused for effect. It certainly produced one.

Johnson gasped, "And if I win?"

"If you win, you get to tie me up," she moved her lips closer to his ear, hot breath cascading over his neck, "and do anything you like to me. For free."

Johnson bolted upright in excitement nearly throwing Spice from the bed. She forced him back down and set the cards between his nipples. Johnson nervously flexed his hands over the deck seven times before cutting. He turned the card over – the Queen of Hearts. He lay back on the pillow, evidently satisfied with his standing.

Spice smiled and pushed her breasts towards his face as she drew her card. The Ace of Spades. In one lightning-fast motion she flashed Johnson the card and handcuffed him to the bedpost.

Watching through a peephole from the adjoining room, James Vagabond nodded his approval. All was going according to plan.

Spice now shackled Johnson's other wrist to the opposite pole and began removing the remainder of his clothes. Johnson was clearly enjoying himself. Too much so to notice Cherry enter the fray. Adorned in a transparent orange kimono with soft sky blue playsuit underneath, her head crowned by an elegant bun with two extraneously large needles jutting out at right angles. She smiled at the scene as Spice finished binding Johnson's legs with rope to the two posts at the foot of the bed. Tossing an opaque black handkerchief over Johnson's face, Cherry kissed him full on the lips as it wafted down over his eyes and she proceeded to fasten it into a blindfold. Spice ran her tongue up through his chest hair and whispered "Trust me, you'll feel more this way" before tiptoeing out the door.

Cherry Waters removed her kimono and held it out as far as her arms would stretch. Taking her time, she lowered the garment until it only just tickled Johnson's toes, barely grazing the skin. Shuddering in delight during the eternity it took to reach his knees, involuntarily straining at his bonds – kicking, jerking– as she drew it up, up, up. Over his heart she passed the frock back and forth, left and right, ever slower as sweat began to gather at his temples. Johnson gasped and made to speak but she quieted him with an even lighter finger to his lips. As she danced the fabric over his face, hair carried smoothly out into its folds, his breath altered, settling into enjoying himself, but she knew the visible tension in his body would soon be screaming for release. The delicate silk began its way back down, minimal contact, minimal touch. Upon reaching the feet again, Cherry stretched the kimono out over Johnson and let it fall, snatching it a fraction of a second before it reached his torso. The breeze thus provided sent torrential shivers right through him.

An old inkpot sat atop an oak dresser in the corner of the room and Cherry removed the quill pen sitting in it. Again with merely the slightest of brushes, she ran its feathers up the sole of his left foot, from heel to toetop, before moving up his calf. It was only on the third circuit of the plumage, following the road mapped by the silk, that Cherry saw fit to begin her questioning.

"So tell me, Mr. Johnson..." Cherry smiled as she sensed an electrical charge spring to surround his skin, the animal awareness that something's not quite right. "...why are you here?" She let silence linger a moment. "In Cleveland?" And now leaning in and over, a long lick of his right hipbone preceding the question. "In 1918?"

"Why you..." Johnson was thrashing violently, ferociously, yanking at his handcuffs, stomping at the ropes, wild shakes of the head attempting to remove the blindfold. Cherry waited patiently until he had tired himself out.

When no answer was forthcoming, she slowly knelt by the side of the bed and began tumbling the tiniest of breaths over all his most agitated parts. With gasps - made all the more piquant by the squeals, giggles, and moans she superfluously emitted along with them - and hovering hands tracing figure eights over stomach, hips, and thighs, those infinity symbols reinforcing how long she could keep this up, knowing he couldn't, Cherry stood steady over Johnson's lapsing body as he twitched and spasmed, writhed and screamed.

Again holding a finger a millimetre away from his lips, flicking it in and out of his mouth as he raged to bite. "Shh, Mr. Johnson. You know what happened to your other Jonson, don't you?" She shook her head sadly for her own benefit then sent a stream of air tumbling straight down his torso.

"Or do you?" She swept the kimono again from neck to knees.

"Well, it wasn't pretty." Letting the cloth fall over his crotch and sweeping it up at the last second.

"Not like me." Letting her palm actually stroke his abdomen this time, as Johnson shrieked in agony.

"Don't you wish you could see me…again? Perhaps if I raise this blindfold…" Cherry lifted the covering momentarily, letting it snap back down before his eyes could adjust to any meaningful sight.

"If you'd only tell me where the time machine is, I'll let you go. You see that, don't you? Don't you, Mr. Johnson?" His throat emitted the sound of a sewer draining and Cherry laughed quietly to herself. "I'll let you go and you can satisfy yourself to your heart's content."

A gurgling began to rumble just below his epiglottis. Something was trying to make its way out. "Ssss…sssss…sxxxx…sixty…."

"Yes, Mr. Johnson?"

136

"Sixty-nine!" He panted excessively, like a dog rollerskating through a hurricane. Cherry waited, lips and brow knitted. Finally he spurted, "Sixty-nine Brewer Street."

James Vagabond was up and running. Cherry, her faculties heightened by the extravaganza, could sense him racing down the steps of The Red Garter. She turned her attention back to Johnson. "Now, if you'll kindly wait while my colleague verifies this information." And with that she sat at the edge of the bed, just close enough for Johnson to know she was there, and began sharpening her fingernails with an ivory emery board. It was a good thing James Vagabond was by now outside, it would've broken his heart to hear himself referred to so. Not even as a 'drinking buddy' but simply a 'colleague'.

But in actual fact he was now racing back into the cathouse, having no idea where 69 or any other number Brewer Street was located. With her knowing smile Mama Overcast pointed the way, "Clear across town, love. A right and a left from The Shining Armory."

James hurried back out into the street, searching in vain for a cab. And then searching his pockets in vain for any money with which to take a cab. The cash Cherry had received from Foxy remained with her. He took a deep pull from the whiskey bottle he'd grabbed from beneath the sheets and thought for a minute. What would Arthur do?

In no time flat, James was prying open the door of the Robert Graves Funeral Home. Quite simple to break into as most thieves did not attempt to burgle these sorts of establishments. He snatched the keys to a hearse off the rack and was on his way. Once he zeroed in on the car door the keys corresponded to, James was beset by another problem. There was no steering wheel in this motor vehicle. Nosing around the front seat, wondering how Americans guided their automobiles or if they even did at all, soon his head banged against exactly what he was looking for, hidden in the dark shadows on the far end of the compartment. "How extremely odd," he commented to the starter pedal. But it would have to do. He buckled his whiskey bottle into the seat and walked around to the driver's side door.

Sitting on the wrong side of the car reminded him that Americans drove on the wrong side of the road. Or was America like Argentina who changed from left to right in 1945 and being now before that time in 1918 as he was he'd have to adjust back to normal? James decided not to risk it, aiming for the middle and hoping for the best. It'd been a long time since he'd driven himself anywhere and luckily the amount of drink in his blood veered him from the middle to the correct lane. Even more luckily, no one else was on the road. Soon James brought the swerving hearse to a stop in front of the address Johnson had given to quell Cherry's torture by caress.

Trying the door to number 69 Brewer Street, James found it to be locked. He walked around the side of the building, peering in through the windows. It didn't look like anyone had been in this place for quite some time. A layer of dust attested to this. James pushed on the glass and the window gave with ease. He quietly lowered himself in and down.

Inside James was now confronted with rows of giant covered vats, similar to the ones he had seen Daniel Jackson brew beer in, only much larger. But something seemed odd to James. As a counterpart to the ubiquitous dust, there was also an absence of any smell of alcohol. He rapped his knuckles absentmindedly against the metal side of one of the tubs, pausing to ponder the tinny echo he heard in response. Aha! This must be an actual real life disused brewery, he considered, stopped in its tracks with the advent of Prohibition. He had yet to see one of these with his own eyes, despite all the venues he'd visited still producing the supposedly illegal alcohol.

This has to be the place, James sensed, trying to call on his detective skills whilst keeping the visions of lively vats previously invigorating the premises from interfering with his judgment. And possibly owned, at least in the era he now found himself, by Johnson's employers, who would hopefully be revealed to Cherry soon. But scouting the scene, James could find no clues whatsoever as to who this organisation might be. A door at the far end of the room opened into what must have been an office in the not-so-distant past but James saw nothing that would even point to a lead, just empty drawers and cracks in the walls.

James felt the pressure of time now. If he couldn't find the time machine here, if in fact Johnson had been lying, he'd better alert Cherry as soon as possible in order for her to extricate the information before Johnson went completely round the twist. James wondered how long he would last under similar circumstances, especially with Cherry doing the stances.

On his way out of the office, James noticed a curious outline on one of the vats. Investigating further it looked as if a large rectangle had been burned through with a blowtorch. Big enough to walk through even. A door, perhaps? James pushed and was astonished by what was confronting him. Amidst the faintest bouquet of Pilsner, barely scentable to the naked nose, reflecting in the moonlight from a small aperture at the top of the vat was the silver shape of a United States telephone booth. James could hardly believe it! He began sniffing the air wildly in celebration, trying to approximate the fumes-induced drunkenness he'd experienced with the venerable Mr. Daniel Jackson. The very man who had ordered him to stay put this evening. James' sense of urgency heightened further, he made a quick examination of the contraption. But he could see nothing more than an exact replica of the machine he himself had traveled in. With that irritating ordeal in Florida preying on his mind, James hurried back out the window, leaving it slightly ajar for their return, and hopped into the car. He sped the vehicle back behind the Robert Graves Funeral Home, unbuckled and grabbed his bottle of whiskey, and, keeping the keys to the car, ran back to The Red Garter. It would've been too risky and sad to park the hearse in front of that establishment.

Sprinting up to his earlier position at the peephole, the previous view to a thrill was now downright horrifying. Johnson was on the brink of insanity – bawling and sweating, fluids sluicing off him as his body shook uncontrollably. In between the wracks of pain were momentary respites filled with begging and whimpering. It was obvious Cherry would get no more information out of him. James sounded the agreed upon wolf whistle followed by three quick raps on the wall to let her know that Johnson had been telling the truth. As Cherry half-turned to acknowledge this, the look on her face told James she had been unable to extract any information on Johnson's employers.

Cherry's hand, suspended in a faux-grip above Johnson's stomach, paused and relaxed. Throwing her right leg over the agonised man's body, James heard her say "Okay."

Now straddling Johnson, she reached for the keys to the handcuffs and the look of frenzied hope that washed over not just Johnson's face but through all his muscles and seemingly out into his aura made James feel sick. As the metal bracelets fell loose, Johnson groped wildly and blindly. Cherry remained fiercely upright as his torso sprang verticle, arms locking around her back, pulling her into him, satisfying his lust his only concern. Beating his to the punch, she pulled out one of the giant needles from her hair and thrust it deep into his back, piercing his heart. As Johnson slumped away, Cherry slowly, with dignified carriage, got up, removing and wiping clean the weapon. Slipping back betwixt kimono sleeves, she cast cold eyes at the body on the bed before emitting a slender smile, pleased by this variation of death by caress.

If there had been any doubt in James' mind as to why Cherry opted not to eliminate Johnson at Arthur's funeral, witnessing this brutal slaying now removed all trace of it forever, along with any lingering misgivings from his guts as he vomited copiously into an empty drawer in a bodily attempt to eradicate what he had just seen. James stared into the puddle of sick, recognisable only from the strange behavior of others, Vagabond himself never having thrown up in his entire life. But he had no time to fully register the shock. Rinsing his mouth with whiskey and spitting it, out of respect, into a different compartment of the dresser, James rushed to the room next door where Cherry embraced him in victory. It happened too quickly for James to fully enjoy the physical contact or even realise what was happening, he was quite astounded by the power he could feel coursing through her and still more than a little in awe of the viciousness he'd just espied on display. Cherry, practically flying now, raced down the stairs, pulling James along behind her.

It wasn't until they were halfway to Brewer Street that the two finally spoke. James - held in check by the immense energy streaming off the radiant Cherry - cleared his throat not once but twice before querying, "By the way, how did you dispose of the time machine you used?"

Cherry gazed out the window and very matter-of-factly replied, "I pressed the self-destruct button." She tapped a sprightly triplet rhythm again the car door. "Then ran."

The hearse came screeching to a halt. James had never felt more sober in his entire life, despite the two plus bottles of whiskey he'd put away today. "What?"

"The self-destruct button. Now come on, you silly man, we've got a mission to finish."

"What self-destruct button? No one told me about a self-destruct button. Why on earth would there be a self-destruct button in the first place?" James' mind was reeling. This was all too much. First witnessing cold-blooded murder, now he's informed he could have inadvertently touched something in the machine that would have blown it, and him, up! And what if this had happened whilst traversing the very fabric of time? What wider implications would that have had? What could that befuddled Professor have been thinking?

Cherry remained perfectly calm, almost uninterested. "That's odd. D knew about it. If you press the star, zero, and pound signs all at once, twice in a row, the machine will explode in thirty seconds. Now drive."

James did as he was told. Why hadn't anyone told him? But it was no use pondering why anyone in the Service did what they did, or rather neglected the things they did not do. He put it out of his mind. "Well, we can't use that now."

"Why not?" But her mind was only half on her question. Her body surged with strength and those dark eyes burned magnificently out into the night.

"Because it's in the middle of a warehouse, inside a giant empty metal vat. We can't afford to destroy any property. Especially if it might belong to Johnson's employers."

They soon arrived at 69 Brewer Street. With James keeping watch, Cherry - adrenalin still flooding her system from her kill - hauled the phone booth from its resting place out and into the hearse. James felt a combination of sheer admiration – was there anything this beautiful woman couldn't do? – and the need to act so he wouldn't be diminished in her eyes. Admitting he'd drunk nearly three bottles of whiskey today wasn't going to cut it. He'd have to think of something, but for now he wasn't going to get in Cherry's way after what he'd just seen her do. They silently got back into the hearse and set off again.

After a few minutes, Cherry turned her head and asked, "Where are we going? We can't take this thing back to The Red Garter." James cocked an eyebrow and Cherry continued, "Well for one thing it's not a customer. And if we were to use it there as some sort of futuristic playroom, the self-destruct button could all too easily be activated."

James' muscles tightened, he still wasn't over the shock of that news. "We could put it in a coffin back at the funeral home? Or even just bury it in the graveyard?"

"A coffin? Really? Don't you think that might further traumatise the already aggrieved if they were to open the lid and see that? Burying it…wait, stop, stop!"

James jammed on the brakes and the hearse jilted to a halt. Cherry sprang out, hauling the phone booth under cover of darkness to an awaiting pond in the park below. James confusedly withdrew from the car, picking up the discarded kimono, and watched Cherry now wading waist-deep, dragging the machine down towards the depths. He heard her gasp for air – always arousing to James' ears – and watched her disappear below the surface, bubbles rushing to replace where the silvery box had just been. James thought of Cherry's sister and her enticing tattoo. Had it not been for a breeze carrying a distinct hint of lime, perhaps the source of all the citrus that kept appearing in James and Cherry's drinks, James might've lost himself in reverie. An ethereal finger seemed to be scratching at James' subconscious. What was it trying to reveal? Frustrated by the itch, James looked up to see Cherry's dripping wet heavenly body – the soaked sky blue playsuit now perfectly see-through - rising out of the shallows. She was nonchalantly singing Marlene Dietrich's 'Untern Linden, Untern Linden' to herself. James swallowed, a gulp that could've drained the entire pond thrice over. The sight pushed all thoughts of Bubbles Waters, as well as anything else, from James' mind. And as he patted his perspiring face with her kimono, it suddenly hit him like a keg falling from on high. Nocturnal visions begat nocturnal visions and James ecstatically recalled that spark from the edge of sleep some nights ago.

Driving back, James could barely contain his excitement. "Cherry, I had a dream the other night. I've been trying to remember it ever since. It was important." He looked over to make sure she was paying attention. She was. "Glimpses keep coming back to me. Not of the events of the dream itself, but the fact that the vision was there, waiting to be returned to. And I think I've got it now. A way out of this whole mess."

Cherry swung towards him, her wet hair splashing his face like a jet of the finest champagne. He'd piqued her interest, if only because this was the most she'd ever heard this agent say at any one time. "And?" she prompted.

"I was standing on a hill, similar to the one up past that very pond. And I was holding a giant balloon in the shape of an elephant." He paused for dramatic effect. "On it were painted the words 'Stop Prohibition'." He glanced over at her.

"That's it? That's your whole plan? A balloon?"

"It may have been a kite." James shook his head clear, remembering more vividly now. "No, no, it was definitely a balloon. It's trunk reared up and out, searching. Made of papier-mâché, don't you see? Paper?"

"It was made of paper but it wasn't a kite?" Cherry's withering look would have stunned him had he not been too focused on verifying his vision to see it.

"That's not what the paper meant. And when I let it go, it carried me, by further invisible strings, up, up and over the Sourpuss Estate."

They soon returned the hearse behind Robert Graves' Funeral Home and, after Cherry refused James' offer of his grimy coat, walked back to The Red Garter in silence, each lost in their own thoughts. They were quickly shocked out of these when upon returning to Cherry's room Johnson's twisted death grimace greeted them, staring up from his lifeless body on the bed. But having been over the years hardened to such surprises when trying to accomplish anything, James simply shrugged his shoulders and set off again for the undertakers, leaving Cherry to bring the corpse to the curbside. Which she accomplished by hoisting Johnson over her shoulders, carefully traversing the window sill, and stealthily climbing down the outside of the house, knowing Mama Overcast and possibly others would likely by waiting in the parlour downstairs. Stashing the stiff in the bushes, she scaled back up to her quarters, dried herself off and, thinking of James, playfully changed into an identical sky blue playsuit. Grabbing a warm fur coat she again whisked down the wall and waited for Vagabond to bring the car around.

As the hearse turned into view, Cherry heaved Johnson into her arms and ran to meet it. She had the body in the back before James fully stopped the vehicle. Vagabond had the sense she didn't really need him; that she could have carried the cadaver to wherever she chose its final resting place to be.

"Where will it be then?" he queried, genuinely curious.

Cherry sat thinking, the barely audible click of her tongue against the roof of her mouth driving James wild. "Let the water wash away his sins." James closed his eyes and shuddered as she pronounced, "To the pond."

Leaving her fur coat in the passenger seat, Cherry Waters again lugged a heavy load down towards this secluded little lake. James did not register that she had changed her apparel or that it was even now dry, his imagination supplying the already glimpsed visual delights underneath. Soon she resurfaced - the dazzling slippery vision that had shocked James into remembering his grand plan – having sunk the bloody body into her namesake. Sensuously sliding her hands over and around each other, again and again, she shrugged, "Simple enough. The door was already open so I just pushed him in and flipped the machine over."

They arrived back at The Red Garter just in time. Cherry grabbed a bottle of brandy and headed off to relax in a hot bath to relieve the chill that she knew must be in her bones, however obscured by adrenalin and bloodlust. James had barely downed two shots of whiskey before Daniel Jackson walked through the door.

"Ah, James. The very man I've come to speak to. I see you've been keeping yourself safely out of sight this evening."

James gulped as his eyes opened wide. He hoped it appeared non-committal.

"Now this fella that's been asking about you -"

"Daniel," James began, not quite knowing what was going to come out of his lips, "I believe Miss Cherry's, um, taken care of the situation."

Jackson gave a quizzical look, but was not surprised.

"Yes, she, uh, called in some favours. And he's off searching in all the wrong places, on the other side…" James coughed, "…of the world by now. He did seem a bit wet behind the ears when it came to the detective game."

"Well, James," Jackson clapped Vagabond on the back, "I know you must be dying for a drink. Let's head on over to Camelot. And if what you say is true, I suppose you won't be needing this to walk the streets." He pointed to a clown costume with a jackal head mask that he'd evidently brought with him. Though as the two set out, James couldn't help but notice this disguise remained in The Red Garter. Vagabond wondered if it would see some use tonight after all.

After James had calmed himself with Campari and Calvados, the events of this evening playing havoc with his palette, a deep pulsing from within alerted him to the fact that the time was nigh to broach a delicate subject with Mr. Daniel Jackson.

"Daniel, I think I've seen what we need to do. Now, stay with me on this. Is your man Evan Scent capable of producing an alcohol that is, to put it bluntly, tasteless?"

"Now James, I daresay we've been very good to you here. I know the English do things a bit differently but - "

"No, no, no, Daniel. You know I love your booze and all the wild varieties and concoctions I've found upon these shores. Even if you people kccp putting limes in them for some unknown reason. Please don't take offence. Listen…" And James explained the stratagem his subconscious had gifted him.

By the end, Jackson was nodding towards victory. "Alright, good sir. We shall begin work on the morrow. And now I'm off to bed."

James, less shaken but still needing to be restored, had no intention of curtailing the night just yet. "Daniel, I've had a long - "

146

"Ah yes. All cooped up in that cathouse."

James' eyes flickered to their outer perimeters. "I was thinking about heading back to The Red Dragon. There's a man there who just might be able to help us."

"Whatever you say, James. Password tonight for a single gentleman such as yourself is 'Hans Olow'."

"Excuse me?"

"Hans Olow. Mickey's idea. Friend of his from home, I think. Good luck, Sir James." And with that, Daniel Jackson strode confidently out of Camelot.

Rushing into The Red Dragon, eager to bolster himself up before his current wave crashed towards the shores of sobriety, James yelled to Mickey, "One of everything!" But the barkeep was too far away to hear Vagabond properly above the din of the dauntlessly delusional. Fortunately this gave James the time to realise what adulterations these drinks might contain. As Mickey moved closer, James changed his order to "Three Red Dragon's Eyes, two gins, and a boilermaker."

While Mickey repeated these back to him, James searched his pockets but could find no money to pay for the beverages. Looking down at the floor in consternation, he saw Nicholas Quarterly there, the very man he'd come to find.

Nicholas for his part was still attempting to lift himself up from having fallen five minutes before, but he kept getting distracted by half-formed brilliant ideas, losing them as he patted his person for any sort of writing implement. He looked up, covering one eye with his palm, and squinting hard with the other. "Hey, I know you," pointing to the empty space to James' right, then left, then straight at him. "I owe you some drinks."

James smiled and pulled Nicholas to his feet and once steady on them again, Quarterly produced a wad of bills. "Won it on a horse named Throwaway. Placed the bet years ago, gave a few bucks to an Irishman, and he's only just paid me this evening. Still, some flowers take forever to bloom." He slapped money onto the bar and exclaimed, "As many whiskies as this will buy. For myself and my friend here."

Mickey did some quick calculations and set about pouring each man three shots, this being the purchasing power of the cash after Mickey had deducted what Nicholas already owed him. James hoped Nicholas would remember another call to work before he could finish his allotted three.

"How's the writing going, Nick?"

Nicholas looked down into his liquor. "It never ends. I got somethin' due in the morning, no idea what it is." He made his signature sweeping gesture, James being quick enough to lift all six shotglasses before they were knocked off the bar.

Vagabond threw back two whiskies at the same time, noticing how efficient this method could be. He moved closer to the swaying Nicholas for privacy as well as to make sure he'd be heard. "Listen, Nicholas, I know you write fiction. Have you ever thought about creating your own news? A form of fiction come to life?"

13 – Sucker Punch

"This is it! This is the one!" Evan Scent shouted triumphantly.

Daniel Jackson lifted his dark goggles, peering up from behind the complicated set of bubbling tubes and gurgling funnels. "You're aware that's the exact same synthesis we had two days ago?"

James Vagabond nonchalantly pushed over a bowl of champagne sorbet, one of many such flavoured ices lying about to cleanse the palate between tastings. "How long have you been too drunk to notice the difference?"

Evan Scent smiled sheepishly. "About two days."

It had been a little over forty-eight hours since Dr. Chicago had paid the make-shift chem lab a visit, delivering six gallons of ninety-five percent pure medicinal alcohol in a stuffed polar bear, and promising 'there's more where that came from'. Legally restricted to providing a 'patient' only one pint every ten days, Chicago blatantly ignored this precept whenever he could. He was cautious, however, and Daniel and Evan were required to scribble initials next to three dozen names on a checklist. These appellations Chicago had copied off tombstones all across the city shortly after the dry laws had come into play. He had yet to be questioned over such practices but should the case arise, the good doctor's plan was to remark that no one had informed him that so-and-so had passed on, and then pour the puzzled official a drink in fond memory of the dead. With Chicago's help, Evan, Daniel, and James found the perfect odourless potation on their third attempt at altering the medicinal liquor. However, this did not stop the four men from testing plenty of other specimens over the next two days.

After all had been decided and a large quantity of the tasteless tipple cooked up, Cherry arrived carrying something even more ominous than the engagement ring on that same hand.

"Like it or not, you're going to have to see how it mixes with this stuff," she announced, setting a pail of Vine-Glo down on the table. After much grumbling and perhaps only because Cherry was wearing a black leather body suit unzipped halfway down her chest with no brassiere on underneath, James poured some of the new spirit into a glass of the grape juice. He grimaced, holding this mask of pain until he could physically bear it no longer, his body automatically instigating a swallow. He closed his eyes and nodded that it passed muster. Cherry scooped a cup of Vine-Glo for herself, tasted it, added the new mixer, sipped again, and satisfied that all would be well, zipped herself up and was on her way.

Nicholas Quarterly soon knocked on the dilapidated door to Daniel Jackson's basement, having somehow navigated the perils and pitfalls of the floor above.

"Nick! What are you doing here?" James Vagabond asked, startled by the intrusion, but buoyed enough by experimental byproducts that welcomes were warm all around.

"I was walking back from handing in a piece on the Hashek pirouetting badger to a new Nature column in some paper or other. No idea if this thing actually exists or not but I'm quite pleased with the writing. Composed it right there in The Dragon, even with that young redheaded fella with the cowlick smoking all that opium right next to me. It's not just a mixer anymore. Then I saw Cherry a little ways down the road and she told me where I might find you, but to come alone, and keep it secret. I can see why. What have we got going on here?"

Evan, with effervescent pride in his work, began talking Nick through the distilling process and copiously feeding him the juice of their labours. Quarterly was visibly impressed and kept reaching for his notepad to jot down what he was witnessing until finally Daniel confiscated pen and paper. Nicholas repeatedly insisted he again be shown how they arrived at such a flavourless façade and the four men began tests anew.

Hours later, after the quartet had finished dancing a rhumba to an imaginary soundtrack, it dawned on James. "Gentlemen, forgive my manners, but it appears I forgot to provide proper introductions. Nicholas Quarterly, this is renowned craftsman Daniel Jackson and our gifted chemistry-inclined friend, Evan Scent. Daniel and Evan, meet Nick Quarterly. He'll be helping us out with the mission."

"Hic! I will?"

"Remember everything I explained to you the other night? That's what all this is in aid of."

"Even better, good sir! Count me in. Again. One two three fff-" And as the other three picked up where the rhumba had left off, Nicholas jolted in an attempt at attention but slipping, collapsed bottom-first on the grubby cement floor.

"You boys have fun extraneously experimenting?" Cherry smiled as Nick and James joined her in the back room of The Round Table.

As they settled into their mostly liquiform meal, a thought poked at the periphery of Nicholas Quarterly's memory and he inhaled deeply. "You know, James, Miss Cherry, I heard the most curious report when I was at the office yesterday. Cold-blooded murders at three different New York City police stations, all within a couple hours of each other. Interests us as these cops were all sympathetic to our cause. My good friend in the city, Oliver Shout, went down to the crime scenes and said they were gruesome. The look on the men's faces…" He shook his head in an effort to clear the spectacle Shout had described.

"What happened, Nick?" Cherry prompted, sensing danger.

"It seems that a man – and this is strange right from the beginning, no one could recall exactly what he looked like, only agreeing that he moved lightning fast and the general impression was one of a blur…"

Cherry gripped James' thigh under the table, Vagabond feeling that by now familiar but uncomfortable cross between eros and extreme concern, as they both realised who was most likely behind this.

"The first victim was a man I knew, vaguely. Met him my one and only time in New York covering the Celtic Beers of Great Britain festival. You would've loved it. I was intrigued at first by his bowler hat and skills at throwing the b.s. around, and as I got to know him, I learned Officer Deskjob could put back pints with the best of them. Sad to see him go."

Nicholas choked back a sob. Cherry placed a comforting hand over his and he continued, "According to all accounts this mysterious visitor was polite to a fault and at each station he presented the same spiel. Seems he'd invented some kind of device that when the user breathes into it, those in authority will definitely be informed of whether or not there is any alcohol whatsoever in the subject's system. Of course the force has to keep up its pretence of agreeing with these ridiculous drinking laws so when he offered to demonstrate how his new contraption worked, they humoured him."

"An Officer Duke and an Officer Hazard followed my old friend Deskjob into a backroom at their precinct. The stranger handed each of them a small pipe and urged Officer Duke to blow into his. The gentleman then held the pipe up to show a marking that read zero percent. How he would've known that the previous evening was Duke's first night off drinking in months is anyone's guess. This guy then produced from his satchel four cans of unmarked beer, assuring the brass that although he knew it went against everything they believed in, it was necessary for the cause of justice that they partake of this - in the grand scheme of things - tiny amount of toxic alcohol. Only then could they see how the apparatus worked and how it would shape the future."

Cherry stole a covert quizzical glance at James.

"Hazard made a show of being cajoled into drinking the single beer he was offered and once he'd exhaled into the gadget, all looked to see a reading of 0.02%. Deskjob finished the remaining three beers rather quickly. The unidentifiable inventor, someone peeping through the glass reported, then smiled and instructed Deskjob to 'blow hard'. The next thing anyone knew, Deskjob was falling to the floor clutching his face and the mystery man was gone! Officer Duke and Hazard had also collapsed to the floor. Sheriff Jalapeño rushed in and found the device still stuck in Deskjob's mouth, metal pincers piercing both his cheeks."

Cherry shuddered. James too could not repress a wince.

"The autopsy revealed that Deskjob was killed by a lethal dose of opium. Industrial-strength glue found on his lips. The doctor conjectures that with the adhesive placed on the outer rim of the contraption, when the victim 'blew hard' it activated something that ejected the hooks through the cheeks. Whoever did this wanted to make sure the device would stay in his mouth at all costs. The attempts to breathe would become more and more desperate as opium flooded the system. It was so cleverly designed that even if the first breath didn't result in immediate death, the panic that would surely set in by the pipe being stuck to the lips, not to mention the pincers, would bring about near-instant hyperventilation. Not long would be needed for enough opium to get in and finish the job."

James Vagabond whispered to Cherry, "A sort of deathalyser test." And Cherry, obscuring the facial twitch with a covering hand, giggled despite herself, just to break up the horror of the tale.

"And what's more," Quarterly continued, "Duke and Hazard were also pronounced dead, each having been shot in the ear with a blowdart containing curare. Paralyses the respiratory system, don't you know. The killer obviously keeping to a sick sort of theme. He got Chief Inspector Hale using the same methods at his next port of call."

They sat in silence for some time, each staring into their beverages until Nick's pushed on his bladder too urgently to ignore. When he was safely out of earshot, Cherry placed a reassuring right hand on Vagabond's forearm. "Well, it seems he's in New York. Maybe not for long, but at least we'll be safe for the party this weekend."

James nodded hesitantly. He agreed with Cherry but wished for her touch to remain a moment longer. What could Hoo-Nose be doing in the Big Apple?

On the day of the next Sourpuss soirée James Vagabond made it a point to sleep late. This would minimise the number of hours he'd have to go without a drink. At four p.m. he wandered over to The Red Garter to be tidied and dressed, stopping en route to urinate in an alleyway and let all his resentments concerning the grooming flow out of him. Rounding the corner back onto the street, he soon passed a park and almost stopped in his tracks. Over on the grass a father was attempting to untangle a small child from a gigantic sprawl of string. At the end of which, the father wending and weaving it through the loosely knotted maze, was a red kite. The boy's sister stood by watching, eating an ice cream cone and holding a blue balloon. James' courage was greatly bolstered by the sight.

It was only during the trimming of his beard that Vagabond panicked, running from the room and throwing back a secret shot of gin. Although it didn't make the hair and dirt grow back as he hoped it would, the refreshing juniper did bring him a little closer to getting used to the idea. As the lint was being brushed off James' tuxedo and he stood staring at the unfamiliar reflection in the full-length mirror, Daniel Jackson entered the room carrying an ornamental box.

"I wish I could say I wish I could join you, but there's no way I'm staying sober for anywhere near that long." Jackson announced, punctuating the statement with a lingering pull off a longnecked bottle and a further stretched sigh of satisfaction. "Ahhhhhhhhhhhhhhhhhhhhhhh…" He proceeded to reverently open the case at which point a warming glow filled the room, lamplight dancing off the three silver flasks within. "Sir James-"

Vagabond felt the compulsion to kneel. Instead he patted under his arm where he'd slipped on his trusty holster minutes before.

"This was the good Miller's personal flagon. Snuck deep into enemy territory on many an occasion and used to celebrate his most notorious conquests, whether they were sexual, of a political bent, or even just over the malaise at break of day that keeps some rooted in bed." With great ceremony Daniel presented James with the largest of the containers sitting in the chest. Vagabond received it with extra care, attentively placing it within the secret sheath hanging below his left armpit. Turning again mirrorwards, he took a moment to practice a few quick draws. Daniel then strapped the smaller two vials to each of James's legs at socktop height.

"Do Arthur proud, James. Word has just come in that bigwigs from far and wide are coming to this shindig. Leaders from Prohibition Introducing Suitably Sinless Practices Obliging Our Republic and Prohibition In Several States Providing Our Unending Righteousness just rolled into town. Delegates from Prohibition A National Treasure Service have already been dehumidifying the air here for coupla days now. I trust you'll put an end to all these bad ideas this evening."

At seven p.m. Nicholas Quarterly and photographer Gordon Flash met James Vagabond in the entrance to The Red Garter. Daniel Jackson was busy securing a mini-barrel of the flavourless moonshine underneath the floorboards of their awaiting vehicle. Working on the assumption that most of the attendees this evening will never have taken a drink in their entire lives, James didn't think it would need much to get them going. But Daniel was supplying backup just in case, knowing full well that he and James would drink the reserves later themselves if the barrel didn't end up being used. Cherry kissed James on the cheek and wished him luck. Blushing shamelessly beneath his neatly groomed beard, Vagabond settled into the backseat and they were off.

The journey to the Sourpuss estate was nerve-wracking for James Vagabond. He found he could not stop flexing his right hand, the one that would be responsible for getting the liquor into the Vine-Glo. And he'd have to do it as quickly as possible without calling any attention to himself. It didn't help that Nicholas Quarterly was amiably passing a bottle of whiskey back and forth to Gordon Flash. Although Nick wasn't imbibing at his usual alarming rate, James found the pendulum-like procession of the bottle agitating rather than soothing. The booze producing a certain self-awareness, soon Nick turned to James, "Just let me know if this bothers you, old boy."

Over Nick's slurping swig, James informed him, "I've never asked any human being, or animal for that matter, to stop drinking and I'm not about to start now."

As they pulled into the gigantic Sourpuss driveway, Nicholas and Gordon stretched themselves out on the floor of the car. Once Mitch had parked in a safe spot, James took a deep breath and walked nonchalantly to the front entrance. The bell rang out into the eerie silence of the night and soon the sounds of locks turning and clicking preceded Mrs. Amaretto Sourpuss' face peering around the corner of the opened door. After she'd looked every which way to make sure that James had come alone, Amy Sourpuss threw her arms around Vagabond's head exclaiming "James! How wonderful to see you!" and kissing him forcefully on the cheek, ran her tongue up, around, and in his ear for much longer than James could hold still for. As she reached his lips, he pulled his own back into his mouth and cleared his throat.

"Do come in," Amy offered, adjusting the bottom of her dress and once again regaining composure. Fanning her face with her hands, she let Vagabond slip ahead of her. As James turned back at the entrance to the ballroom he caught Amy staring at his behind and lasciviously fingering the velvet rope blocking off the staircase to the upper levels of the house. He thought with horror of what alcohol might do to this woman. But still he must serve.

"Go ahead, James, I'll be with you in a minute."

Passing the statue of Brother Kenneth Tapp on his way into the designated party area, the scene was much the same as James remembered from the last gathering. Careful to always keep an eye on his objective – the punch bowl sitting on the banquet table – he espied sombre ice maidens sitting primly on the sickly beige couches and divans, trios and quartets of stiff men standing in stiffer suits, and of course duos circling the room in military rigidity inspecting the proceedings and looking ready to court martial the slightest offence.

"I say, you. Man." James looked over to see Gustav Witheredspoon either having a mild heart attack or beckoning to James to join them. Vagabond risked on the latter. When he reached Witheredspoon and Featherbottom, he was greeted with a simple nod from the former, Featherbottom eyeing his companion with slight suspicion.

In deep, harsh tones, at odds with the schoolgirl gossip he was emitting, Featherbottom launched back into a tirade that had been going on for some time. "Would you believe it? On Tuesday, Jetski was actually caught jaywalking red-handed, or should I say red-footed-" He paused to see whom of the party appreciated his tomfoolery which would thus give him permission to laugh. No one did. "My apologies. I know I shouldn't joke about such grave matters but the officer on duty went straight up to him, the report stating that Jetski then uttered the 'S' word. And I don't mean 'Cincinnati'."

James examined the look of shock crossed with pleasure that was now creasing Witheredspoon's features. As this subsided Witheredspoon put in, "Yes. I heard our gracious hostess Mrs. Sourpuss revoked tonight's invitation before Jetski even made it back on the sidewalk. And Marketcrash has spent the last two days out in the shed with him, administering the punishments."

Vagabond, keeping a poker face, recalled something Daniel had read to him in the papers just the other day. The fact that since the dry laws had been passed, minor crimes such as swearing, mischief, and vagrancy, had all gone down. The article mentioned nothing about the fact that people still drank and excessively at that. He smiled inwardly that although he'd been sleeping in the alley behind

The Round Table most nights, he'd yet to be picked up on any charges.

At this point Amy Sourpuss snuck up behind him and James felt the presence of her hand hovering over his buttocks shortly before her fingers pulled at his jacket sleeve.

"James, dear, there's someone I'd love for you to meet. The leader of a wonderful new splinter faction, the Party Incorporating Supreme Sterilising Prohibition Over Our United Realm, Mr. Desmond Spot."

Desmond Spot made no attempt to acknowledge the introduction or even move any part of himself in the slightest. Wondering if the man was still alive, Vagabond acted quickly. Nodding to Spot, he turned to Amy. "If you'll excuse me, Mrs., I mean Amy, I've got a tickle in my throat-" Sourpuss' cheeks reddened considerably at this and Vagabond summoned all he had to finish the sentence "- I'm just going to help myself to…some punch."

But Mrs. Amaretto Sourpuss would not be so easily avoided. She followed Vagabond to the banquet table like a lovestarved puppy. As he steadied himself to pick up the ladle in the punchbowl, Amy brought a quarter of a cucumber sandwich to her eager lips. Mesmerised by the physique in front of her, she squeezed the bread too tightly en route and a great gob of mayonnaise shot out onto the slope of her right breast. James did his best not to pay any attention to the situation but as he averted his gaze, Amy proved impossible to ignore. Wiping off the condiment with deep powerful strokes which in turn tugged her cleavage down even further, Sourpuss shouted, "James! James! Would you look at what I've done? Can you believe that? All over my-" She stuck her chest out in James' direction, staring back and forth between him and her bosom as if trying to conjure him into providing the words. "….my new party frock, James." Still continuing these eye movements, "It looks as if I'll have to go upstairs all alone and get undressed…and then get dressed again." She was disappointed at the outcome of that sentence.

"A shame, Amy. It's a very nice dress."

The two stood staring dead into each other's eyes for a full minute. Frustration growing too great, Amy finally stormed off, breaking the deadlock. James sensed that now was his chance. A door upstairs slammed and as all eyes followed the bang from above, Vagabond whisked out Arthur's flask, spinning the cap loose with his forefinger as he flipped it over and emptied the contents into the punchbowl. Time seemed to slow down and as he returned the container to his holster the volume of the crowd increased, all wondering aloud what could have provoked the thunderous outbreak. Not a single soul was concerned with James' activities. Letting out an enormous sigh of relief, James scooped himself a cup of Vine-Glo and contentedly sipped.

After a few such servings, the sobriety of the past few hours pleasantly washed itself away and James began to feel more like himself again. The only problem now being that he was the only one anywhere near the banquet table.

Vagabond's senses heightened from this integral part of the mission now being accomplished, he quickly noticed the fireplace over by the hideously hued couches. It was worth a try. If they get hot, they'll drink to cool down. Marching over to the brick façade he quickly began making a show of looking for a way to open the chimney flue. There wasn't any wood around, this being a summer evening, but Vagabond remained confident inspiration would come to him. How he longed to break those degrading portraits of imprisoned bottles out of their frames and toss the whole lot into a burning, purifying heap but he knew calm and steady was the way. Poking his head into the hearth and staring up into the darkness he heard a soft female voice intone, "Oh you English eccentrics." As he pulled himself out from over the grate, concern starting to set in, he noticed quite a crowd had gathered around him. Not only that, he promptly twigged, they all had glasses in their hands.

And soon, at first almost inaudible, James heard the first sound of mirth. So light it was almost a sigh, but rolling within minutes, like a sneeze that triggers an avalanche, into outbreaks of shy giggles succeeded by chorused titters. The overall harmonic structure of the room, given body by those high ceilings, approached something like that of decent human civilisation. Men and women began to mix, speaking to each other for the first time in years.

Back at the banquet table, in between sips they could not possibly guess the consequences of, a half dozen Prohibition supporters began sampling the victuals on offer.

A gasp was followed by the intrigued, "Are you...are you eating a strawberry and an orange...together?"

"Well...I suppose I am."

"Rather strange, don't you think?"

"Oh. Oh yes. Ha ha."

"Here, strapple this on."

"Oh. With an apple now. You beast."

Soon a stout preacher with a handlebar moustache was dipping a pig's trotter into a crock of honey.

"I say, what are you going to call that one, Father Theodore?"

As this minister tore off a bite, complete with extra slurps, he considered the comestible in his hand for a moment. "How about a Trotsky Honeymoon?"

"My my. How weird. Hey! What about watermelon and deer?"

Near the fireplace, guests began to act as if a blaze had indeed been lit. Outer garments were shed, hesitantly at first, and then more quickly, with an air of not wanting to be cognisant of their actions. And even though hot blood was now racing, this did not prevent this cluster from huddling closer together, as if for warmth.

Vagabond strolled about, keeping an eye on the punchbowl whose level was growing dangerously low. Witheredspoon came up to him, stopping to wheeze and slap his knee, his red face looking like it might explode at any moment. "I say, old man, Featherbottom and I are going to throw some eggs at Marketcrash and Jetski in the shed. See if we can't time it so that one lands underneath the whip right before it cracks down. Care to join us?"

But Witheredspoon and Featherbottom were laughing too hard to care much if James answered, so busy were they pointing at each other, slapping shoulders, and miming the actions of tossing an egg and thrashing it to pieces. James snuck away back to the banquet table.

"I don't think that's finished yet," he called to a servant lifting the punchbowl. And as James scooped the remaining dregs of the Vine-Glo into a cup, a new bowl miraculously appeared in place of the first. He knew he must act quickly, but how? Already those who had emptied their glasses were sloppily making their way back for more. James swirled the fortified grape juice around in his mouth, letting it roll over his tongue and slide betwixt back teeth. It still tasted terrible. The knowledge of its potency just happening to be tricking his taste buds into accepting its presence in his mouth. Calling him back to the moment, something bumped into his right foot from underneath the tablecloth. Squatting down immediately, both to investigate and instinctively protect the flasks strapped to his shins, he came face to face with a voluptuous strawberry blonde tumbling about with a pot of cream stolen from the spread above. She giggled when she saw James and, sucking the dessert from her forefinger, brought the digit to her full lips. "Shhhhhh…" she teehee'd again, kissing said fingertip before placing it on Vagabond's open mouth.

Another slam of a door erupted from beyond the ballroom entrance and this delightful lady laughed "Oh!", scurrying to the opposite end of the table and poking her head out to catch the action. James, without consciously registering what he was doing, his sight still focused on the rear view of this beauty on all fours, pulled off both mini-flasks from his legs and sprang to his feet. The back-up supply was mixed into the new punchbowl before anyone's eyes left the main doors.

A furious Amaretto Sourpuss, in a hastily thrown on change of attire, marched back into the party and up to James Vagabond who was casually stirring the punch and scooping himself out a cup of the old 'Glo. After glowering at James for a full ten count, she snatched the glass out of his hands, and stomped off swigging.

By now the get-together was in full swing. Reasonably justifying its appellation as a 'party', people were dancing, laughing, and making out. Vagabond kept circling, eyes constantly checking the punch but, even with all he'd had to imbibe of it, the contents of this second bowlful remained fairly topped up. His calculations on how much liquor would be needed to get these people going were bang on and he as yet saw no need to return to the car for reinforcements. Besides, he shuddered to think of Amy following him out into the wide open night.

As James swept back by the fireside, he noticed a few of the ladies had started to kiss each other. And soon some of the men nosed their way in as well. As tongues twisted every which way, there couldn't be a better confirmation that the punch was indeed working. The chain of bodies grew ever longer and James was even surprised to see Mr. Desmond Spot making his way towards the action. Surprised until he sensed a slight disturbance in the air.

"That's my wife! Unhand her this instant!" Desmond Spot leaping into the fray, hands outstretched to the throat of an unsuspecting gentleman. Tackling him off the couch and into the laps of another similarly engaged couple, they were momentarily separated as the interrupted lady kicked them to the floor. Dodging the continuing stomps, the assailed raced round the couches. Spot, arms spread like a giant bat, diving over the amorous action, and landing with a thunderous thud on his victim. As he rained blows down upon this hapless gent's face, Spot looked back to cast a withering glance at the woman this man had been kissing. It was not his wife.

162

Violence raced into the air. A heated debate over the artistic merit of the colour scheme used in 'Ungenial Bottle in Prison Number 42' now giving way to pushing then shoving. The glass hatchet whisked off the podium, umpteen paws grasping for the handle as this sculpture-cum-weapon slipped betwixt loose limbs. One frantic individual finally seizing it only to have his murderous intentions thwarted by a Trotsky Honeymoon landing smack on his pate. As the syrup dripped down his cheeks, two ladies sprung from their entanglement on the divan to lick the nectar from his face. The hatchet dropped and was kicked clear across the room into the midst of a bombastic food fight. Oysters swiped through hot fudge stuffed down necklines, Witheredspoon and Featherbottom launching hard-boiled ostrich eggs skyward without any regard to a target, flying half-eaten donuts approximating a psychotic game of horseshoes. More than one partygoer was running for their lives to escape a chicken carcass destined to enclose their skulls. Ham considered by far the most amusing weapon being wielded, the sonorous qualities of its slap against skin providing unending satisfaction for a sextet of octogenarian matrons.

Father Theodore, furious now that the ingredients for Trotsky Honeymoons were nowhere to be seen on the table, began grabbing passersby, lifting them full off the ground by their lapels, and demanding to know why this person had stolen such foodstuffs. Dodging curveballs of fricasseed rhino, freshly brought back from Africa, as well as yak ribs boomeranging about the place, James stumbled into an impromptu rugby match. Scanning the four corners of the room he could not catch sight of Amy Sourpuss anywhere, wondering how she could possibly be tolerating such destruction of her home. He dove out of the way just in time as four of the matrons ambushed the scrum, hellbent on recovering the ham being used as the rugby ball. Sliding through spilt bouillabaisse, a mess of bodies were heading straight for the banquet table. James clocked the procession and was racing towards the punchbowl as if his life depended on it. For reasons known only to themselves, Father Theodore now had Desmond Spot in a headlock and whilst twisting his neck was also attempting to rip off what he believed was a toupée. Spot, on the other hand, had retrieved the food-fouled hatchet, the sculpture now in both hands raised maniacally above his head. A second before the skidding crowd, crazed preacher, P.I.S.S.P.O.O.U.R. leader, and glass axe all came crashing into the table, Vagabond leapt, and as a moment's grace bestowed itself into this carnage, the punchbowl landed within his open arms just as he came crashing down upon the hard wooden floor. Raising the oversized chalice to his lips, he polished off the remainder of the concoction as he attempted to stand.

No sooner was James on his feet than being swept off them again, pulled into the ardent embrace of a trio of ladies whose hearts had raced that much faster at witnessing his heroic action. It was just as well. As his form disappeared back down into the couch, Spot and Theodore soared straight into the dish, knocking it into the fireplace. Having served its purpose it shattered into a thousand pieces, the two men rolling through these with locked limbs and wild abandon, neither sure any longer what their objective was.

Despite enjoying the overeager gropings of three women under the influence of alcohol for the very first time, James Vagabond knew it was time to leave. It took some moments to extricate himself but he was finally able to slip away without too many tears to suit and eyes. Maneuvering through this shambles of decorum, he finally saw what had been keeping his hostess busy all this time. Legs wrapped around the bronze statue, Amy Sourpuss – head thrown back, dress half-off – was writhing in ecstasy, licking the face of Brother Kenneth Tapp and screaming, "James! Yes, yes! Oh, James!"

As he strolled out into the entrance hall, Nicholas Quarterly, chuckling and scribbling with great mirth, paused to clap James on the back and hand him a bottle of whiskey. Gordon Flash was busy catching the bedlam on film. "Well done, James, well done."

"What are you doing here?"

"After watching from the window for a while, we reckoned no one would give a damn if we got a little closer. I think we're about done anyways, whaddya say Gordo? Let's head back to the car."

Moving triumphantly out into the night, a hysterical giggling greeted their ears. Peering into the shadows hovering close to the house, James saw two hunched figures shaking with uncontrollable laughter. Witheredspoon's voice called out "We've occupied the bushes, old boy!"

Pushing their way into the expectant atmosphere of Camelot, James and Nicholas shouted in unison "Mission accomplished!"

Wild cheers erupted, fresh drinks poured as the ones in hand were downed in celebration. Cherry rushed up to James, kissing him again on the cheek and, as she rubbed his arm for what felt like an aching eternity, smiled "Well done."

"Wait until you see tomorrow's papers," Nicholas beamed as handshakes and hearty slaps on the back made the rounds. "That reminds me, three quick cocktails, then we'll have to head to the office, Miss Cherry."

Wading into the midst of a bustling workplace where Nick often flogged his wares, Gordon Flash raced to the darkroom while Cherry set off to find the editor. As she closed Mr. Hautere's door behind her, the big man swiveled around in his seat. She discreetly locked them in and with a mindless-to-all-appearances forefingered twirl of the hair asked, "So you wrote all those big machines out there yourself?" Cherry let her purse containing trusty needles and handcuffs drop to the floor. She had other, less fatal, distractions in mind.

Nicholas jumped onto a table and shouted, "Stop the presses! Have I got a story for you."

14 – Smoke 'Em If You Got 'Em

A sweet smelling fog rolled heavy over the Sourpuss estate, in which a lost Vesper Sparrow sailed dreamily down towards the front steps. Its course punctuated by delirious tweets emanating from the grand spectacle unfolding in its mind. Jarring visions of a distant night where communist Cardinals led by a crazed chaffinch were racing across coastal France to assassinate King Rail and his queen Virginia all the while a Jamaican Mango of Flemish descent swooped betwixt cuckoos, loons, taciturn commoners, Old World relatives, Ugandan Cranes, Phoenician gulls, comic marionette-like woodpeckers - no less than one hundred and forty characters in all - to save the day. The enraptured sparrow soon settled itself on the newspaper resting before the Sourpuss door just below the headline 'BOTTOMS UP TO PROHIBITION!'

Although Gordon Flash had produced an excellent shot of Father Theodore brandishing his buttocks to the rest of the guests, adding new weight to his 'Trotsky Honeymoon', Nick and the crew decided against using the photo. In the end they opted for a panoramic sweep of the debauchery, Mrs. Sourpuss' gyrating figure prominent in the foreground. With Cherry keeping Hautere busy, the team worked tirelessly to get the morning edition out, foregoing ego and phoning every other Cleveland paper as well as any known associate across the forty-eight states. Oliver Shout was delighted by the news, as were David Pennymeadow, Sam Picnicbasket, Bob Jacobson, and Eddie The Druid down in Charleston.

Further along the street paperboys sleepily struggled through the dense clouds to deliver other headlines such as 'PROHIBITION BASH', 'P.A.N.T.S. DOWN', and, as one reporter had already run with the Jetski sideline, 'INHIBITIONS SHED AT PROHIBITION PARTY'. A mile away Daniel Jackson was running for his life.

Bursting into The Red Garter and slamming the door shut behind him, Jackson steadied himself against the wall, gasping uncontrollably. It took two minutes to catch his breath and he inhaled deeply. The rush of oxygen to the brain did not help his cause. Collapsing at the foot of the stairs in a horrendous crash, Mama Overcast, Cherry, Sugar, and Spice all came running down alarmed at the sight of a prostrate Jackson, something no one had ever seen before.

"Daniel, Daniel," Cherry shook him forcefully.

Jackson rolled over, delirious. "The angels…the dragons…the serene terrifying beauty of it all…What's happening, James? What indeed is going on?"

Cherry tenderly smoothed the sweat from Jackson's brow. "James isn't here, Daniel."

Jackson bolted upright, shaking. "But…he's nowhere. He must be here."

"What do you mean James is nowhere?" Cherry bit her lip, nervous but resolute.

"I have roamed this unreal city and found not a trace. As if he were a dream." He shook his head frenetically. "Must be here."

Cherry's eyes darted about her in alarm. Out the windows she could see nothing but billowy white and grey. An electric warning zipped up her spine. She cautiously made her way to the door, Daniel screaming 'Nooooo!' as she opened it a hair. An enticing heady perfume greeted her nose and she knew exactly what it was. Opium. A snort from below brought her eyes to the ground.

"Cherry! Are you seeing this? Hyacinth girls playing chess with archdukes. That one just stole his rook. Taxis through the thunder, whirlpools of fire. The pure poetry of it all. I should be writing this down."

Nicholas Quarterly patted his pockets then began rubbing his stomach with wide sensual sweeps of the wrists.

"Nick!" Cherry shouted with joy, with hope. "Have you seen James?"

Quarterly's eyes were now on his fingers encircling his bellybutton. Cherry shouted again, calling him out of his reverie.

"Um...no, no I haven't. Not since we left for the office last night."

In the early hours, when Cherry returned from keeping editor Hautere out of Nick and the gang's way, Vagabond was heading back to his beloved alley for some much needed shuteye. Cherry had kissed his cheek again, congratulating him once more, before rejoining the celebrations at Camelot. And that was the last she saw him.

"Can you get up?"

Taking Nick's slight rolls to either side to be a negative, Cherry proceeded to drag the writer into the relatively safe air of The Red Garter.

"Sugar love, please put Mr. Jackson and Mr. Quarterly to bed and make sure they drink plenty of water. Take care, gentlemen. I'm on the case." And with that Cherry raced upstairs, returning momentarily in a white catsuit. Before she was out the door, Mama Overcast stopped her.

Strolling into the private back room, Overcast soon reappeared waving James' confiscated Colt .45. "Here, dear. I hope you don't, but you may need this."

Cherry swallowed a hearty lungful of air before rushing out into the smoke-covered streets, her right hand clasped firmly over her nose and mouth. She ran past mimes asleep atop a fire engine, with clowns circling about below in great concern, a grounded lead-grey hot air balloon, its expedition party all now occupied pressing flowers betwixt their maps, and a curious parade of men carrying chickens in one arm whilst holding megaphones to their eyes with the other. Presently Cherry arrived at the entrance to The Red Dragon and rapped the three quick knocks. Waiting for a response, she frantically patted her pockets with her free hand as if searching for the password. When the panel finally slid open she desperately tried, "Hyacinth Prufrock." To which, the slat slammed shut.

Counting steadily to forty-seven, Cherry then knocked again and ducked immediately. The peepslot whisked open and stayed so as the eyes behind scoped out the view. Locks turned cautiously and as the jester opened the door an inch to investigate, Cherry pounced. Gliding her tongue into his mouth with effortless ease, swirling, twirling, languorously lingering before pirouetting off into grace, her lingual acrobatics sending pulses of ecstasy down to the man's very toes. When she withdrew the jester fell flat on his behind and stayed there, lost in hitherto unbeknownst euphoria. Cherry shut the door and paused to gulp down the much less opium-saturated air permeating the hallway.

"Mickey, do you still have those German oxygen masks?"

"Vhy Miss Cherry, I've still got nearly the entire stock left." The Finn smiled.

"Give me one. And I may need more."

Donning the contraption and sucking the vivifying gas into her lungs, Cherry sat at the bar wondering what could possibly be going on. It seemed the whole city was enveloped, somnolent and enchanted. There could be only one man behind this. Although she already knew the answer, something inside her made her ask, "Mickey, have you seen my friend James?"

"That Englishman you ver vith? Not since a few nights back. He and that topsy-turvy journalist hatching all kinds of plans. But…" Mickey's arm sweeping across the room, "…is not so uncommon here."

A familiar man in a red cape with a blue suit below stumbled up to the bar.

"Vhere are your companions, Tweety Bird?" Mickey smiled. "Find any vhales to vrestle or did you get caught stealing your 'six thousand apples' before you got to the vater?"

Cherry felt electricity sizzle about her skin. She couldn't exactly say why but she suddenly became much more alert.

"I've no idea what happened to them. It was quite a night last night." Tweety Bird fingered his cape as if offering proof. "When we saw that fog swooping over the shore, they plunged on in at full speed, braying like stallions. Lost them within seconds so I opted to mosey on back. It's eerie out there. Let's hope it lets up soon. I was meant to take my boat out this afternoon."

Recalling their first visit to this establishment, Cherry put in, "That's right. You have a boat, don't you?"

Tweety Bird spun around. "Correct, ma'am. Tweety Bird McCoy at your service."

Cherry and Tweety Bird were soon racing lakewards through the ever-thickening smoke, oxygen masks strapped on, lugging a dozen more between them. The clouds frequently twisting into terrifyingly detailed shapes – sleek muscular dragons whose heads would spin round and round, towering owls with impossibly pointed beaks and sharper stares, empty upside-down decanter forms already breaking apart. Tweety Bird pushed his mouth guard to the side, pointing the way to Cherry.

"Here she is. Carrie Gravy. Clever name for a rumrunner, don't you think? Many a trip we've made together, to the Canadian shores and back. The authorities never question what type of gravy is in all these sauce bottles." McCoy fanned the air with his hand as they stepped on board, momentarily revealing crates of condiments beside satchels of pork scratchings. Tweety Bird continued waving as the fog rapidly covered the cargo again. "You really think your friend is out there? In all this?"

A couple of miles from shore, in relatively clean air apart from a few renegade wisps of narcotic smoke, James Vagabond sat tied to a mast, his arms and torso bound tightly to the pole by intricately weaved and knotted rope. Only his legs were free. All about him, scattered about the open deck, were bottles in various stages of disintegration. James' shoes had been removed lest he try to escape, but the damage to his feet was only a secondary consideration. His torturer knew the psychological effect the broken glass would have on the victim. As indeed the bathing implications of the water beyond. Past this, a solid wall of greyish white whorled at the horizon. A gloved hand scooped a fistful of cocaine from a barrel and blew it into Vagabond's face. James spluttered and, taking advantage of his need to inhale, another grainy cloud followed promptly in its wake. This had been going on for some time.

The voice connected to the hand however, James could not place in one physical location. It seemed to flit all over the deck, unattached to any bodily form, or none James could see. A high-pitched nasal hiss snaked into his left ear, in the next second booming from the far shadows before sliding straight down the mast pole to slither again past his lobes.

"She'll be here soon. And once you have been both taught a lesson – and understand why you're being taught a lesson – you will be discarded. While I simply jump back in that era-hopping device -" A vicious wind swept over James to the bow of the ship. He somehow knew it meant the time machine was on board " - and clean this whole mess up."

Hoo-Nose continued. "It'd be no good to torture you back then, even just a few days ago. You wouldn't have transgressed yet. Or not to such a degree. Your silly games, and that's all they were – shots, to use an analogy suiting your sloppy style, and small ones at that, compared to my exquisitely crafted Nebuchadnezzar."

James wondered if the rumours were after all not true. That instead of abstaining from such vices, Dr. Hoo-Nose was in fact a rampant cocaine addict. Dispelling the thought came another puff of powder and its more potent sequel.

"Small-time aggravations. If only that Johnson hadn't ballsed things up. Nevertheless he was just an unwitting pawn in my game. There to distract you and your little band of merry men and women who thought getting Cleveland to acknowledge its own hypocrisy would somehow save the day. With you wasting precious time, I was busy in the big cities – Detroit, Chicago, Washington, New York – making real progress. Your tiny victories wouldn't have been of much consequence…if it hadn't been for that - " Hoo-Nose's voice seemed to snarl the final word from inside the middle of James' brain " – writer…right in the midst of my operations as well!" The mast shook as if a gargantuan fist had slammed down upon it.

James swallowed, snorting and coughing, attempting to clear his throat of what felt like a gob of chalky goo. "Why isn't Nick here then? If he's the one you're after."

"Miss Waters will be bringing him any minute. Be sure of it. Hear the sound of whatever dinghy they purloined in the distance? He thinks he'll be getting the story of a lifetime with me, but I have other plans. You see, Mr. Quarterly is not really my concern. He would never have amounted to much had it not been for your meddling. It would've been to my advantage to let him linger in the drafts of The Red Dragon until with the advent of the permissive 1960s, old age and rough times would conspire to have him finish a best-selling memoir. Further publicity for my cause."

"But now!" Another thunderous convulsion of the mast. "Now this story has leaked all over these united states, from sea to shining sea. And great as I am, I am humble enough to know that I do not possess the wherewithal to be in all places at once. So once you and the girl are exterminated – with the writer once again watching, as is his wont, before I pen his final 'the end' – I'll set sail back through the winds of time and eliminate you again. Perhaps at the Miller man's funeral, show Johnson how it's done, or maybe that afternoon you lay beside her for the first time."

A wave of longing filled James' chest now, romantic nostalgia lingering awhile. When it had subsided, he smiled inwardly that their plan had worked and would have succeeded if not for the element of time travel now heavily in Hoo-Nose's favour. Vagabond had been taught early on in the Service never to accept defeat – there was always another drop in the bottle if you whacked it hard enough, 'last orders' was simply a call to move on to another establishment where the booze would flow freely, and to always be ready to accept the miracle of an awaiting can greeting you round the corner. He struggled to remain positive despite the fact that everything pointed to a gruesome and unseemly death for himself and the woman he loved.

"You see, James Vagabond – oh yes, I know you, know you well – the cocaine that you can't help but take in will have you wide-eyed and ready to witness my revenge. Even with me being so wasteful." He nonchalantly blew another grainy heap over Vagabond's head, waited until James squirmed and then viciously flicked a fistful into James' face. "Under other circumstances I would never tolerate such squandering, but there is a delicate beauty in knowing that your system – like everything else with you – can't help but suck it in. And with said system suffering from lack of your beloved booze – Ppppphhhh -" Pausing in his rant to exaggeratedly spit. "You people with your *needs*…But this white mosquito swarm will keep your attention to my administrations rapt. And all this I consider only practice."

"One thing I learned on those wretched islands – everyone is too eager. Impatient. In order for anything to work, it needs to be tested. Let go of your attachment to getting it right the first time. One can always transcend failure. Yes, even at the cost of my septum in that wretched blast off Isla del Coco. My beautiful Roman nose.

Surpassing even that of Julius Caesar. The envy of Prince Nez and Digital Underground...shattered by my own hand. Even taking the life of my beloved five-legged dog, Birdy. But the advances made to pharmaceutical knowledge were astounding and my lair was rebuilt quickly enough, away from any prying eyes and sniffing, perfectly functioning..." here Hoo-Nose's voice evinced a wince, a split-second fighting back of emotion "...beaks."

James looked away, out into the smoke-filled sky over the lake, and blinked. He wasn't sure but for a second he thought he spotted a kernel of sun peeking out from high above.

"I know your feelings regarding the cleansing power of H20, Mr. Vagabond. Is that what prevented you from actively pursuing Miss Waters? Afraid she'd have washed you of all other women?" Hoo-Nose cackled and James realised the poignancy of the past tense, the doctor convinced it was now all too late.

The Carrie Gravy sailed silently through the smoke. Cherry and Tweety Bird both focused on controlling their breathing in order to remain calm. Who knew how long they'd be out here and if they carried enough oxygen with them? Cherry emptied her mind of all distraction while Tweety Bird's thoughts danced in the substance-fueled swirl of adventure that was his life. Pushing through the palpable mist, a faint hum caught Cherry's ears. And soon, although the veil thickened, pockets of blue in a horizon beyond began to appear. Vanishing too quickly to be sure of, with Cherry and McCoy casting muted glances at one another – 'did you see that?' – each wondering if perhaps the opium haze had penetrated their respiratory apparatuses.

With ever more speedy swathes of smoke barraging their faces, Cherry yanked Tweety Bird to the floor. Presently, to their panic, a mighty thud announced a halt in the Carrie Gravy's progress. Cherry rushed to the side of the boat. To her surprise a vast area of clear air as far as the eye could see, albeit under an overcast sky, hung almost within arm's reach. It was then she noticed the giant fan whirring atop the boat blocking their way. And the mounds of burning opium in front.

James Vagabond flinched after another duo of cocaine blasts shot into his face. It was difficult to battle, on purely aesthetic grounds, the pleasurable sensation. But fight he must. He took a deep breath and summoned all available authority to his voice. "That's where you're wrong, Hoo-Nose. Nick may have told the story but those people -" For the first time James' heart went out to the partygoers of yestereve "– were just expressing their natural inclinations. The alcohol had simply whisked away shrouds of suppression built up over long, dark years."

Vagabond bit down hard, teeth in a vice-like clench, as the mast reverberated off the Richter scale.

"Hogwash!" Hoo-Nose shouted. "How often does everyone regret their so-called 'natural inclinations' the next day? You with your specialised training have forgotten what it is like for the common man."

"And what of the recreations you deal in?"

"My dear James, extreme dreams and extravagant intensity have nothing to do with natural anything. Upon them my slaves will think they're building a new world, which conveniently, in many ways, they are. And central to the construction is a platinum path leading to my throne."

Cherry Waters stealthily pulled Tweety Bird McCoy up over the side of this strange obstacle. The two undid their oxygen masks, thinking it wise to conserve supplies. Slowly they traversed the 180 degree safe area behind the enormous fan, on the look-out for any signs of activity. If Hoo-Nose was on board, he would've heard the thud and now Cherry's white catsuit, distractingly sexy as it was, did little to camouflage her presence. Staring up into the colossal rotating blades, they marveled at the sheer quantity of smouldering opium before them. Cherry took a deep breath as out of the corner of her eye she saw first one, then beyond that a dozen more similar ships, each sending out smoke signals to those already asleep on shore. Hoo-Nose could have James on any one of these. It was then that Tweety Bird cautiously tapped her on the shoulder and pointed out into the farther visible reaches of the lake where the smudge of a lone ship sat bobbing.

"What is keeping them? But yes, patience, like I said. It will all work out right in the end. What do I care if I must wait hours, days, decades for them to arrive? Get here they will and once I'm through with you, I simply waltz into the moment-mixer-upper and correct for present, future, or whatever mistakes. As I said, you are simply a rehearsal. You recall all the fun you had in that hearse? Well, now it's your turn."

"Once I've rectified your cock-ups, and the coast is clear, I shall have a whole fleet of boats, an armada in the Atlantic, blowing smoke throughout this land of the free. Yes, in case you hadn't gleaned, Vagabond, that is what is happening out there, making this lake ever more spooky. Your companions are presently making their way through fourteen test models I'm pleased to report are doing a valiant job of sending Cleveland off to the lunatic house of slumber. And aside from my satisfaction, all this will be erased when I head back to do the real work, launching my offensive on a grand scale. You'll see, or actually no you won't, such a shame - when the majority of the nation is sufficiently soporified, I will simply stroll in and re-write the Constitution myself."

Hoo-Nose paused to make way for a heavy sense of drama. James yawned. "And what of my employers back in the future, I hear your thoughts screaming, Mr. Vagabond?"

James' cocaine-focused mind however had grown tired of Hoo-Nose's megalomaniacal rant. Vagabond took in the information he needed but parading out of the recesses of his psyche was a beautiful mermaid-like maiden whose figure graced the labels of a certain lambic he had once been called a 'slow drinker' over. He remembered the evening as if it were yesterday, when he spent far too much time admiring the bottle before he remembered he could pour the fruity contents into a glass and have the best of both worlds.

Hoo-Nose hissed him back to the present moment. "Well, the future is mine now!"

With night now falling, Cherry Waters clung to the bow of the ship, having arrived just in time to catch these final words. To her immediate right in bold black letters blazed the name WATER FOWL, except the F had been all but washed away. Motionless, she held tight, listening for her time to move.

"Yes, I shall create wondrous new chemical compounds that will leave the masses ever more depraved. And all one needs to hook them is an initial vision, or even the promise of a first bliss, something, anything that will be transcendent beyond their wildest dreams. Little do they know how much there is in that outer realm of possibility. For the humdrum fantasies they repeat to themselves are born out of lives that are not so wild after all. Ah, Miss Waters -"

Cherry paused, feet now firmly on deck, concentrating on exhaling to rid herself of the surprise at being addressed thusly.

"Where is the scribbler?"

"Who? What? James, James, are you okay?" she called out over the expanse of broken glass blocking her way to Vagabond, sidestepping the question of which she did not understand the meaning.

"Cherry!" James beamed, struggling at his chains. "Cherry, it's here!"

A tremor shot through the mast with such force James thought his spine would crack. Cherry froze in horror at the sight.

"He is fine, Miss Waters. Now I repeat, where is Mr. Quarterly?"

"I don't know. Whatever do you want him for?" Cherry steadfastly keeping all images of Nicholas Quarterly, possibly working on a new erotic novel with Sugar and Spice, from her thoughts.

"He believes Nick is responsible for his downfall." James answered, an air of cocaine condescension to his words.

Hoo-Nose's voice boomed from far away now as if he was out over the waters scanning the horizon for the desired journalist. "Who did you come here with then?"

"I came alone."

The mast shook with tempestuous fury. Cherry's eyes went wide at the look of pain on Vagabond's face as he gritted his teeth to bear it. She slowly, covertly, drew her gun.

Immediately bottles came crashing into the ship's railings with astonishing speed. Cherry let loose three shots before calming her reactions to try to pinpoint the origin of the projectiles. It was no use, although she picked off two mid-flight, all this seemed to do was add to the jagged path to James. The bottles continued to fly, hurtling in from all directions, relentlessly.

"The gun! He's trying to knock the gun out of your hand!" James called, helpless.

As Cherry's eyes flitted about in concentration, an apple suddenly appeared on James' head. Laughter howled from every corner of the Water Fowl. Moving forward, Cherry ducked and weaved through the onslaught of flying glass. She let off one shot at the ropes binding James to the mast. Although successful, out-of-breath hoots and hollers continued to sing out over the ship. The slack thus engendered by the bullet was minimal. Nevertheless, Vagabond set to work rubbing the bonds against the pole in the hope that friction, as it often had, would come to his aid.

Hoo-Nose was gasping for air now. "Stop, stop, the two of you. This circus is much too much. I haven't felt mirth like this…well, ever. You, Vagabond, acting every bit the baboon you are. And you Miss Waters -"

Cherry raised her gun to fire again. A torrent of flasks, carafes, and flagons came flying at her. An emerald decanter made contact with the gun held loosely in her hand. She let it go. And in that instant, with every ounce of energy inside her, she sprinted towards the doors leading below deck. As if guessing her intention, Hoo-Nose let out a demonic "NOOOOOOOO!" and James saw a blur rushing at Cherry's form. The next second the two were toppling down the stairs out of James' line of sight. Vagabond continued to scrape furiously at the ropes.

At the moment of contact, turning with astounding agility mid-air, Cherry slipped her body around and pulled Dr. Hoo-Nose into her embrace. Her lips found his and tongue set to work slipping and wriggling, enticing and teasing, glissading into ecstatic convulsions that shook Hoo-Nose's body with supernatural intensity. Try as he might to pull away, Cherry held fast with everything she had, hands heaving his face to hers, thumbs even caressing where a once Roman nose had been. It was all too much for the doctor. They rolled and rolled along the floor, a ferocious dynamo of passion and delusion, until Hoo-Nose went limp in her hands. Having already spotted the telephone booth concealed behind a large beaten-up poster for 'The Tramp', Cherry dragged the doctor inside, tapped the self-destruct sequence, and ran.

15 – Last Call

Tweety Bird McCoy stood whistling to himself, watching the first hints of sunrise and kicking piles of smouldering opium into Lake Erie. Occasionally he'd lift up his oxygen mask for a tiny hit, something he'd never dare do in front of the beautiful woman who had brought him out here. When she'd set sail in the dinghy for that ghostly ship sitting so strangely in the distance, he'd promptly turned the Carrie Gravy around and headed back for this line of smoking boats. That is what she'd instructed him to do anyways. She hadn't said anything about not loading up the hold with opium. And with that accomplished there was still plenty more to discard; ten more stations stretched out before him. When the blast came, Tweety Bird leaped for the pole of the fan and hung on for dear life. He hoped the lady was ok. Taking another whiff of the fragrant air surrounding him, he somehow sensed she would be.

And soon enough, looking more ravishing than ever in her dripping wet white catsuit, hair slicked back from a face burning with sheer feminine power, Cherry Waters was climbing over the side of the Carrie Gravy and dragging a dispirited James Vagabond behind her.

Tweety Bird adjusted his facemask nervously. "Are you alright?" he asked with genuine concern.

"Yes, thank you." She shook out her hair. "Mr. McCoy, this is James."

Tweety Bird held out a warm hand which James shook wearily.

180

"I say, you wouldn't have a drink, would you?"

McCoy smiled. "You've come to the right place, old boy," and strolled into the cabin below. As he opened the door, Cherry chose to ignore the vast quantities of poppy resin crammed into every available nook and cranny, though opted to don a nearby oxygen mask as the aroma was overpowering. Tweety Bird soon returned with blankets and brandy.

"I was just about to set off for the next one. There are eight more posts to get to but with three of us we can almost triple our time."

Reclining on the deck of the Carrie Gravy after the last of the narcotic pyres had been booted into the lake – Tweety Bird having run out of buoys and waterproof containers long before James and Cherry got there – the three watched as the fans continued to propel fresh air shorewards. It would be some time until the coast was literally clear and there wasn't much point in heading back before then. The city would be asleep for a while longer yet. Besides, McCoy had plenty more heartwarming brandy.

James took another sip as the memory of their final moments on board the Water Fowl involuntarily shook his system. Cherry had come racing from below deck with that familiar electrifying energy, sailed over the arena of broken glass, at the last moment grabbing a shard and slicing him free. They dove over the side and were far below the lake surface when the explosion came.

"Well looky here. All that and not a scratch on her." Tweety Bird McCoy patted the prow of the Carrie Gravy with pride. Docked now, the three were gazing back out into the evening waters after they'd set about sinking every last fan-bearing craft still standing in Lake Erie.

"Speaking of 'all that', Mr. McCoy," Cherry began. "Perhaps the good citizens of Cleveland don't need to know what we went through out there."

Tweety Bird understood the gravity in her voice. He'd never do anything to upset such a woman. He wasn't even sure himself what they'd been through, only that he'd danced well outside the realms of experience he'd thought possible. "Of course, Miss. You can count on old McCoy." And as such is often the way with events of this caliber, the actual details were kept at bay while more practical matters settled themselves in their thoughts. A nice cool beverage was on everyone's mind and they began to walk wordlessly back towards The Round Table.

Passing six separate halves of pantomime horses collapsed on various street corners – even stranger as it was four bottom halves and only two heads – James, Cherry, and Tweety Bird came to accept the state of the city. Further couches and chaise longues abandoned in traffic intersections, finagled into tops of trees, or even balanced on mailboxes seemed the norm by the time they reached their destination. James pushed open the doors and saw not a soul in sight. Had it not been for the pressing question of 'where is everybody?', being alone in a room with an unattended bar would be a dream come true. He set about pouring beers for his cohorts and the three settled in to wait.

"Nick Quarterly, you old soldier!" A baritone voice boomed in time with the slam of a door. Cherry, James, and Tweety Bird stirred, confused, having sometime during the course of the night fallen fast asleep in their seats. Their slumber-encrusted eyes met anomalous half-full beverages left on the table causing them to wonder if they were still dreaming, such waste being rarely tolerated in real life. A portly figure with a thin moustache was poking his rosy face around the back room door. Upon seeing Cherry, this man removed his black bowler hat, bowing as much as his tight black suit would let him. When he again spoke, it was with no less volume.

"Pardon me folks, I'm looking for my old friend, Nicholas Quarterly, but say, you must be James…" The man rushed to shake Vagabond's hand, still bellowing, "Good to meet you, good to meet you. Shout's the name. Did you catch that? FAHAHAHA!" His deep laugh a distant echo of Arthur's. It took a full thirty seconds for the man to recover himself from his joke. "Oliver Shout at your service. One thousand of my heartiest congratulations and thanks to you for saving our great nation."

Oliver Shout tossed a number of newspapers onto the table. Headlines like celebratory squeals burst off the page – 'RED WINE & BREW', 'BARS & STRIPES FOREVER', and 'THE SPIRITS OF '76'. Scanning the text below, James and Cherry were overjoyed at the news.

"…with Pennsylvania, Indiana, Illinois, New York, and Maine joining those states who have raced these past few days since the Cleveland incident to vote against ratification …" James read aloud, pausing to let it all sink in. "It seems there's little hope the Amendment will go through now." He held Cherry's glance for one blissful moment before the picture towards the bottom caught his attention. It was of none other than his old cohorts Jay and Daisy, smiling, secret twinkles in their eyes of passion well spent, shaking hands with important-looking officials. "Florida as well! I knew those two could do it."

Oliver Shout had already helped himself to a round from the kitchen kegs and was busy distributing freshly topped-up glasses. "A toast, my new friends, to drinking!"

"Wait a second there, Shout! Let us get in on that." Nicholas Quarterly beamed from the doorway, ambling through to welcome the big man. Behind him Daniel Jackson, Gwen, Lance, Sugar, Spice, Moonbeam Jim, and the Mark Maker cousins shimmied in, all looking battle-scarred but triumphant. A hopeful clarity was fighting its way into their eyes, through a haze that said they'd seen beyond their wildest dreams.

Everyone was up and embracing. "Where have you been?" James asked to the crowd in general, genuine curiosity mixing with the desire to deflect the same question being directed at him.

"My good man," Nicholas Quarterly slapped James' back, "where haven't we been? I woke up in bed with this fine fellow," pointing to Daniel Jackson, who grinned sheepishly, "the two of us convinced we'd been frolicking through some sort of thunderous lilac wasteland. With Peeping Toms everywhere, made all the more surreal by the fact that when we opened our eyes, ladies' undergarments were strewn about the room as if it'd been hit by an erotic hurricane."

Gwen assumed her role as matron and the Excaliburs began to flow, Lance scuttling across the room carrying them to anxious hands. The Maker cousins soon had Sugar and Spice cosy in a darkened corner. Moonbeam Jim was busy explaining to Daniel and James, "For the life of me, I couldn't figure it out. I was gazing through my hollow stick, penetrating deep into all this smoke, a righteous captain atop his gigantic vessel sailing through the most tranquil of seas. Out of nowhere came a vast processional of frogs, all made of blue cheese, swimming through the air, arms abuzz. I had only to unroll my tongue, which became an enormous flag shuddering in the winds. And like a patriotic canine, I began chasing it and chasing it as it wrapped itself around my tailbone. All of a sudden I couldn't see a thing. Panic set in. It took me the better part of an afternoon to remember this stick has an opaque black bottom and that I'm supposed to be blind."

Faint rumblings tumbled into the back room, growing louder and more boisterous. Cherry strolled out front to investigate, passing the office with its door ever so slightly ajar. Inside Tweety Bird was shouting down the telephone line, "Bill...Bill...it's Tweety Bird...your cousin, Tweety Bird McCoy...you know that new venture you're looking for..."

"One minute," Cherry called to the deafening commotion at the front door. Her hand barely left the lock before bodies toppled through the entranceway, the jubilant parade scooping them back up as it pressed its way into every available space. Strongmen in leotards, bearded ladies in fleur de bois prints swigging from two bottles at once, and pantomime horses, tigers, and bears all carried acrobats balancing barrels on the soles of their feet and tossing cans in every direction. Atop the barrel lids, miniature monkeys were busy banging cymbals, mixing cocktails behind pint-sized bars, and enacting scenes Cherry could've sworn originated in Marx Brothers movies. She peered round the doorway. The crowd stretched off to the horizon, pockets of Dionysian joy exploding throughout a sea of celebration. Carafes were flying over heads in a steady stream of spillage and cheers as they were caught and brought to lips. In the middle distance, second floor windows had been flung open, their inhabitants zealously pouring wine down into eager, awaiting mouths even as they satiated their own. Cherry wandered out into the carousing, surrounded by nothing but smiling faces. She immediately counted no less than six treasure chests opened in the middle of the street, full of dusty dark jars, exotic cruets, and unlabelled jugs with shimmering, almost mystical centers. More trunks, cabinets, and strongboxes were being carried out by the minute. Horses, goats, and cattle pulled kegs on carts ever so slowly through the congregation, their taps flowing nonstop. It was astounding the amount of secret provisions these good people of Cleveland had stored away when the dry laws had come in, even on this block alone.

Having strayed further into the mob than she intended, Cherry was swept up in its effulgent flow. Sailing past unicyclists concocting the seven staged Tibetan Shock Rum, shadowy figures whispering of Rennes-le-Château blue apple brandy, old women whose scarf-obscured faces called out from the farthest reaches of alleyways instructions on where to find the fabled sesame-flavoured Arabian gin, whilst figures all around offered other such rare tipples the likes of which had only ever been rumoured on American shores, Cherry soon found herself in front of The Red Garter. Pushing her way past the interminable queue lunging at the doorway, she espied Mama Overcast counting an overflowing fistful of cash.

"Cherry, love, I'm afraid your room is occupied – quite occupied – and will be for some time. They're commemorating this victory like bunny rabbits. Come back in, oh, say two or three days."

Cherry grinned, obscuring her true emotions, and waved goodbye. She knew deep down that this was the last time she'd ever see this kind-hearted woman. Their work in Cleveland being done, it would soon be necessary to drag James to other fronts in the battle.

Back at The Round Table it was becoming impossible to move. Attempts at a crude human conveyor belt to transport beverages to the back of the room were thwarted by empty glasses closer to the source and the unconscious habit of automatically bringing cups to lips. Newly poured refreshments rarely made it past the third or fourth set of hands. Those gathered by the kitchen door felt a sense of half-remorse at this, even as they themselves were draining those drinks intended for friends further along. Little did they realise the sheer volume of alcohol and cocktail umbrellas carried in by the celebratory cavalcade.

"And after we'd won Palmito Ranch, we danced all night through the sands of that dusty land." James and Daniel found themselves sardined next to a boy of about fifteen who nevertheless was finishing telling them about his heroic exploits in the Civil War. The youth commandeered a beer that was being passed overhead, sampled its contents then shook his head disconcertedly as if to signify his medium-sized sip was quite an achievement. "And did you hear what happened to that Sourpuss lady?"

James' ears, and other body parts too, however involuntarily, pricked up, giving his full attention. "Mrs. Amaretto Sourpuss?" being his first words to this young man.

"That's our gal! Husband's had her committed. Couldn't pry her off some bronze statue except to forage through the house for more Vine-Glo. That stuff, eh? Child's play. In the end he just left a vat of it by her side and called the sanatorium to come pick her up. They carted her and the statue off to a bed at old Bedlam and it seems she couldn't be happier. Wait a minute, there's Sourpuss now. Must go say hello. If you'll pardon me, gents." The youth scuttling off, calling in the direction of a well-dressed man who very obviously didn't know this adolescent from Adam.

"James," Daniel cleared his throat. "I'd like to thank you for everything you've done."

Vagabond made a dismissive gesture. "You should be thanking Cherry."

"I will indeed. She's quite a lady. Don't know what we would've done without either of you." Jackson nodded tenderly and raised his glass.

At that moment a collective gasp seemed to suck the air out of the front room followed by much shouting, applause, and 'huzzah's. Cherry pushed her way through the doors hot on the tail of this lionised messenger. Newspapers were flying everywhere, headlines held up blazing across the top of this special evening edition – 'NONE SHALL PASS!'

Snatching one down, Cherry began reading. It was official. Enough states had decisively voted against the ratification of Amendment 18 that the idea of a national Prohibition was now out of the question. Around her, men, women, and those whose sex was obscured by costume, whether animal or simply outlandish, wept openly, gathering everyone they could about them in a joyous, semi-lecherous embrace. As a chant began to fill the room, sounding suspiciously like Steam's 'Na Na Hey Hey Kiss Him Goodbye', Cherry set off to find James.

Thrusting through the overemotional crowd, she was kissed, hugged, licked, pawed, had sleeve and hair used to dry eyes, pressed, pointed at, shaken, startled as champagne glasses were placed in her mouth, dodging as further flutes headed for other accommodating junctions, and tickled many times over. Amidst the earsplitting whoops and hollers, neigh-ing, moo-ing, and roar-ing from those staying in character, catcalls, whistles, and moans bellowing so low they seemed torn from the other side of consciousness, was the wonder of it all. Mouths spurting 'what have we done to deserve such good fortune?'

"Do you think it has anything to do with all that smoke and us being asleep for two or three days?"

"Who cares? Never look a drunk horse in the mouth, that's what I always say."

After what seemed an eternity, Cherry sidled up to James, beaming. "Have you seen the news, soldier?"

"Incredible, isn't it?" James swallowed a hefty gulp to block his emotions cascading out. "Thank you again for saving me back there."

Cherry winked, driving James crazy. "Let's hope it all affected the future just fine. Speaking of which, the past is a nice place to visit but…we'd really best be moving on."

Daniel Jackson jostled his way towards them carrying six Excaliburs. "Miss Cherry, there you are. My eternal gratitude for allowing our amber waves of grain to shoot ever upwards."

"Any time, Mr. Jackson. But speaking of waves, James and I really must be taking our leave. Thank you for your wonderful hospitality but we should've been back in England ages ago."

"Nonsense!" butted in Nicholas Quarterly, squeezing through the throng. "We've still got plenty more years celebrating to do. This is a time of great happiness. The war to end all wars is behind us, Wall Street has become a world financial leader, and with Prohibition now stopped in its tracks, the future is looking rosy indeed!"

Cherry and James fought to keep smiles on their faces, each not wishing to admit to themselves that they secretly hoped this would be true when they arrived back in the future.

"Say, have you heard what happened to Father Theodore and Desmond Spot?" Nick continued. "Those two are now the best of friends, thick as thieves. Last seen with bottles in hand rushing off to some remote mountainous island intent on joining the revolt there against Colonel Blancmange."

"You! Man!" A familiar throaty voice was heard above the hubbub. Gustav Witheredspoon jovially pushed his way through the multitude without much concern for the crushed feet, slammed shoulders, and whacked waists left in his wake. He clapped James on the back. "That was quite a night, old boy! We held those bushes until well past the cock's crow. Good times, good times. Look who we've found too." He pointed to the flushed-faced figure of Marek Jetski stealing a drink being passed overhead with devilish glee, a look of delight in his eyes that James recognised as the supposed sinner anticipating future self-retribution.

"Turns out Jetski had quite the supply of sauce buried in the old shed. Marketcrash hasn't left its confines for days. Somehow dug the stash up, heaven knows what punishments the two of them were devising out there. Featherbottom's sleeping one off back in a place you're probably not aware of. I think they call it The Red Garter. Don't quote me on that..." Witheredspoon's attention wandered as Sugar glided past. "Well hullo!" She considered herself rather overdressed in a garment that might cover a doll at a stretch but Gustav was taken in even without being aware of her usual fashion sense. He set off on her tail, tongue wagging well past his chin.

Cherry pulled Vagabond close, steadying him as he went faint at her touch. "James, we really must be moving on."

The two looked about them. They seemed far from any conceivable exit and in every direction stood friends they'd be remiss not to say farewell to. Tweety Bird's companions from The Red Dragon had rejoined him, the three now busy holding Marek Jetski's legs up over his ageing, sagging body and funneling whiskey straight into his mouth as the old man performed a handstand on a rickety table. Mitch stood by recounting his own version of events at the Sourpuss estate in which his driving played a much more prominent role in the nation putting down Prohibition than previously considered. Eager ears took in the chase that ensued when Mitch slammed on the gas, propelling his passengers out of the vast circular drive, pursued by sober assailants in one of those new war machines, the 'tank', materialising out of nowhere whilst simultaneously just managing to outrun a ferocious party of ninjas on horseback throwing swords, stars, and psychic maladies in their general direction. Moonbeam Jim slipped through the crowd and playfully poked James in the eye with his stick.

"Have you noticed those two?" He pointed towards Gwen and Lance, their fingertips and glances lingering a little too long as Gwen passed the young waiter new rounds of brimming beverages. "Seems the tiniest sparks…"

"Jim-" Cherry began, placing her forearm on his shoulder, Moonbeam's stick shooting up from the waist as a grin sailed from cheek to cheek. "We've had a lovely time, but James and I really must be going."

"I won't hear of it," bellowed Daniel Jackson, approaching with eight full Excaliburs to hand and a ninth balanced atop his head. "You are, after all, the guests of honour."

And so it continued. Propositions of goodbyes firmly shot down and momentarily forgotten as fresh festivities arrived anew. Even as he laughed and embraced his dear friends, James' inner self raged with conflicting emotions – sorrow at having to leave, the fervent wish to keep celebrating what was a most noble achievement, the gnawing necessity of remaining in the service of DRINKS and thus getting back to the future as quickly as possible, all the while countered by the sheer baffling idea of departing from somewhere where drink was flowing freely.

Long after another sunrise had swept its way to evening, nature finally exerted her influence on these hardliving bodies, sending them crumbling off to sleep. Cherry nudged a drifting James and quietly indicated the slumbering forms of Witheredspoon, Sugar, and Spice cuddling in the laps of the zonked out Mark Maker cousins, Gwen and Lance delicately enfolded in each other's arms by the kitchen door with Jetksi collapsed on top of Tweety Bird on a nearby table, and Nick, Oliver Shout, and Daniel Jackson all propping each other up, empty glasses to lips, quietly dreaming on their feet. Besides the two British agents, only Moonbeam Jim was still awake. He lifted his dark glasses and winked, waving a small oscillation with his stick as Cherry and James departed through the front doors.

They ran through the heaped snoring souls littering the streets, knowing not where, but determined to make the most of this brief respite. Again unconsciously guided by the heavenly body that had bestowed his Prohibition-smashing plan upon him, James accelerated into the path of moonlight spread out ahead.

They soon found themselves at the edge of a field, a shadowy shape at its center emanating faint engine-esque rumblings. Without quite knowing why, Cherry grabbed James' hand and they ran on towards it. The biplane came sailing across the ground, a mustachioed figure at the helm lifting his flight goggles as he approached and asking 'You folks need a lift somewhere?"

Cherry and James turned towards each other, eyes bulging in delighted surprise, before scrambling into the front seat.

"Name's Orville. Now where can I take you two?"

The airbourne journey was excruciating for James Vagabond. He had tumbled into the plane first, obliging Cherry to take her place, quite nonchalantly, on his lap. Most agonising was Cherry's serene smile as she sat with her arm around him, occasionally shifting her weight all too slowly on his thighs. It would be impossible to pretend there was a set of controls or even rogue joystick in this forward cockpit. It was only after they were well over the Florida state line and preparing for landing that James' mind found a distraction from the pressure. Looking over the side to the ground below, he thought he recognised this stretch of brush. Shaking up dust in the shadows of a large palm tree was a familiar car, bouncing furiously, and once again James sent out his silent thanks to Jay and Daisy for their help in the battle of the booze.

Upon landing, Orville graciously handed over three bottles of wine, saluted, and was on his way. Uncorking one, James set off quickly, quaffing the Burgundy as rapidly as his legs were kicking, attempting to work out the kinks of the flight from his body. After a minute of spasms he stopped and called back to Cherry.

"I'm afraid I haven't the foggiest where I left that blasted machine."

Strolling confidently over to him, Cherry smiled warmly and once again took James by the hand. "It's over here, silly."

The two set about uncovering the phonebox-shaped mass of branches and leaves that only a man experiencing the twin effects of time travel and sobriety could possibly have thought hid anything. Finishing their last bottle of wine in record time, James and Cherry each took a deep breath and walked into the telephone booth, James' eagerness once again getting the better of him. Before Vagabond could even realise what was happening, Cherry was hanging from the roof, attempting to situate her body within the narrow confines of the time machine. She wrapped her legs around James' waist and let go. Wrenching the door shut and throwing one arm around Vagabond's neck - his face now firmly ensconced in her cleavage - she punched in the relevant date on the number pad. The position was unbearable for James. His only consolation was that consciousness would soon be obliterated. And momentarily, it was.

'Not another bath!' James' disembodied thoughts first observed and then slowly but sharply sensed water being splashed over his face, accompanied by a woman's screams. Mind and body united again, he struggled to lift his head and open his eyes. A pair of lips were attached to his, and as he falteringly regained consciousness, James recognised the figure of Foxy J. Michel reviving and arousing him in equal measure. He sat up in the shower looking frantically about for Cherry but was swiftly distracted by the fact that Foxy appeared to be wearing only two thin pieces of string, her taut body sectioned into thirds. Miss Michel pulled James out of the tub, simultaneously thrusting a beer into his hand, and led him into the living room where Cherry was reclining on the sofa. James' eyes were drawn to where she held a tall, cool cocktail, her engagement ring glittering in the pronounced Florida sunlight.

"Finally," she laughed. "C'mon, we've got to get going."

"But...but you're not going to stay the night?" Foxy's eyes filled with tears. James turned to Cherry, silently pleading.

"I just spoke with D. We're wanted back in London."

"But what about the effects of time travel? Hasn't everything been altered?"

"Strangely enough, no."

"Well," Foxy began counting on her fingertips, "there was always a one in...muh-muh...muhmuhmuh-" mumbling something James and Cherry didn't quite catch, "...chance of that happening."

Cherry shrugged. "As a sign of their appreciation, some of the bigger brewing companies have chipped in and booked us on a cruise ship back to London leaving in a few hours. D says there will be a bottle of champagne in the cabin as a token of his thanks. Cheap bastard. And we're sharing a room too."

James gulped, nearly sucking his throat down into his chest cavity. The sunbeams off Cherry's ring pierced through his pupils down into his soul. How unfair compensation can be sometimes. You save the world and what do you get for it? A bath and surely cheap bottle of bubbly.

Each was lost in thought as Foxy drove to the port in her cream lime convertible. James couldn't even begin to process the magnitude of what he and Cherry had just been through. Sleep was what he needed and he planned on staying in bed the entire crossing back to London, sailing down the trash chute if necessary should Cherry's proximity prove too much for his fragile heart. Miss Waters on the other hand, whilst pleased with a job well done, mentally reviewed the mishaps of the trip, like any good agent, to be all the more aware for next time. She wondered if there would be a next time. They'd had orders to destroy 'that blasted machine', as James had put it. Foxy would take care of that, and as far as Cherry knew, Professor Welles was still at large. Foxy focused on the road, careful not to let her emotions override her sense of duty.

After a long impassioned kiss, complete with gropes a-plenty, James looked deep into Foxy's tearful brown eyes. "I'll miss you." He averted his gaze shipwards, not wishing to see this beauty cry, and received quite the shock upon turning back and witnessing Foxy and Cherry locked in the same intimate embrace. After whispering farewells, Foxy waved and was gone.

As they walked up the gangplank Cherry turned to James and smiled. "Well, we did it."

James stopped in his tracks, frantically searching his mind and nether regions for what actually occurred during the time travel itself. Surely he would've remembered if... But then he realised what 'it' referred to. "Ah yes, Prohibition." He returned her smile faintly.

Having no baggage, the two made a beeline for the upper deck and its free bon voyage cocktails. After imbibing what should've been enough to fortify even a small army after such an arduous journey, the ship's horn sounded their departure from port. But James Vagabond couldn't be bothered to wave goodbye to this strange land whose denizens insisted on tossing slices of lime into his drinks. He announced he was tired and heading off to check out their cabin.

"I'll come with you," Cherry offered.

Opening the door, they were greeted by a small room with two twin beds. D's slender bottle of what on closer inspection proved to be sparkling wine stood innocuously on the dresser. James sighed. The porthole was wide open, letting in a salty breeze. Flopping himself down on the mattress on the left, James' sleepstarved drooping eyelids shot wide open as Cherry turned to him and smiled, licking her lips.

"I guess I won't be needing this anymore."

She quickly slid off her faux engagement ring, tossing it through the porthole into the depths below. Already kicking off her boots and unzipping her catsuit, she hung the 'DO NOT DISTURB' sign on the cabin door, where it remained until long after they'd pulled into Southampton.